Damselfly

a novel

Chandra Prasad

SCHOLASTIC PRESS | NEW YORK

Library of Congress Cataloging-in-Publication Data
Names: Prasad, Chandra, author.
Title: Damselfly : a novel / Chandra Prasad.
Description: First edition. | New York : Scholastic Press, 2018. | Summary: Indian-American teenager Samantha Mishra, her best friend, Mel Sharpe, and the other members of the Drake Rosemont Academy fencing team are on their way to Tokyo when their plane crashes on a jungle-choked island, so while they hope for rescue, the teens will need to use all their ingenuity to survive the jungle, the old man who is stalking them—and each other.
Identifiers: LCCN 2017026553| ISBN 9780545907927 (hc)
Subjects: LCSH: Airplane crash survival—Juvenile fiction. | South Asian Americans—Juvenile fiction. | Survival—Psychological aspects—Juvenile fiction. | Interpersonal relations in children—Juvenile fiction. | Best friends—Juvenile fiction. | Islands—Juvenile fiction. | CYAC: Survival—Fiction. | Aircraft accidents—Fiction. | South Asian Americans—Fiction. | Interpersonal relations—Fiction. | Best friends—Fiction. | Friendship—Fiction. | Islands—Fiction.
Classification: LCC PZ7.1.P697 Dam 2018 | DDC 813.6 [Fic]—dc23
LC record available at https://lccn.loc.gov/2017026553

10 9 8 7 6 5 4 3 2 1   18 19 20 21 22

Printed in the U.S.A.   23
First edition, April 2018

The text type was set in 13-point Perpetua MT Std.
The display type was set in Viva Beautiful.

Book design by Mary Claire Cruz

FOR MY THREE FAVORITE BOYS:
BASIL, NIKI, AND ALEXIE

ONE

IF YOU'VE NEVER HELD A FAKE EYE IN YOUR HAND, I'LL tell you what it looks like. It's made of glass and feels cool and heavy in your palm, like a big shooter marble or a stone from a cold stream. It's not a perfect circle, but egg-shaped. If you tap it, you'll hear it's hollow inside. The black pupil is painted on, and so is the iris. As for the white part, it's not true white. Tiny squiggles of pink give it a bloodshot look.

I clenched the fake eye in my fist, so hard my hand hurt. This I knew, and nothing else. I had no idea how I'd gotten the eye in the first place, why my clothes were dirty and soaking wet, or what I was standing on. Why was it so green and squishy? Looking around, I didn't know where my old world had gone. The brick, slate, and stone of Drake Rosemont Preparatory Academy were nowhere to be found.

I took a tentative step, then winced. I was aching everywhere. I had to vomit, too, but I didn't think about that as I looked around, mouth open like a dead fish. I was in what looked to be a jungle. The vegetation was thick, lush, impenetrable as a wall. I pushed away vines, mossy branches, and leaves the size of manhole covers. I closed my eyes against prickers and thorns, but when the branches snapped back like clawed hands, I opened them again.

"Mel!" I yelled, tears starting to stream down my face. I felt so confused. So lost. But if I could find Mel, everything would be all right. My best friend would know where we were and what to do.

Desperately, I looked in all directions. What struck me immediately was the violence. Everything seemed to be choking something else: Creepers twisted around brambles, brambles around vines, vines around trees. Every plant vied for space and the thin shafts of light that pushed through the greenery overhead. But there wasn't enough space for all of them.

"Mel," I screamed again, my throat scratchy and raw. My brown school oxfords made sucking sounds as I walked. I felt as if I were being pulled down, as if the jungle might consume me.

When my foot landed ankle-deep in mud, I was forced to stop and try to pull myself together. What I needed was some water. I reached for my bottle in a side compartment of my backpack, then realized I wasn't carrying anything. I had nothing but the clothes I was wearing—and the eye. This fact panicked me even more. I didn't know how to function without my cell, my iPad, and my laptop. They were as much a part of my everyday life as my toothbrush.

My head started to pound. I took some deep breaths. I tried to think of what Mel or her father, Mr. Sharpe, would do.

They would tell me to look for landmarks.

"Okay, fine," I said aloud, just to hear my own voice, something human and normal. "Landmarks."

I looked for exceptional things through the haze of green,

and I found them: a particularly knobby tree, a cluster of red flowers, a huge, stand-alone fern. I tried committing these things to memory. But I'd never been much good at orienting myself—that's what my phone's GPS was for—and my concentration began to trickle away with the sweat that poured off my skin. The truth was, I was too freaked out to concentrate.

It didn't help that dozens of mosquitoes were following me. Swatting did nothing. They bit my hands, face, legs, hair part, and ears—whatever naked skin they could find. I began to scratch the itchy bumps, but stopped when I realized how many cuts and bruises I had. The blood that streamed down my shins incited a new wave of dread.

What the hell happened to me?

"If you can't find landmarks, then at least walk in the same direction," I said aloud, my voice quavering. But which way? For the life of me, I couldn't remember Mr. Sharpe's advice on telling direction without a compass. Something about true north and the length of shadows? Something about where moss grows on trees?

"Damn it, Mel. Where are you?" I desperately needed her to make things right.

Suddenly, I tasted vomit, acid-sour on my tongue. It came up fast, hot, and wretched, a torrent that washed away my shock. As I wiped my mouth, it finally hit me what had happened: Our plane had crashed. I began to remember details: where I'd been sitting in the cabin, where my teammates had been sitting, how I'd been reading some tabloid and listening to music. I must have drifted off—we'd been in the air for hours—and didn't remember going down. I must have blacked out the screams, the terror, the frantic voice of our pilot on the intercom. That was the only explanation. And now I was on the ground, lost in a jungle, my teammates and friends nowhere in sight. Maybe they were injured. Maybe they were dead.

My last iota of courage vanished. I crumpled to the ground and covered my face, a feeble attempt to block out both the mosquitoes and my own fear. I'm not sure how long I stayed like that—ten minutes, maybe twenty. When I finally opened my eyes again, I was numb. Though I was sixteen, I felt younger—younger and helpless. What got me back on my feet, finally, was a glimpse of the landscape ahead. The packed greenery thinned a little, giving way to trees. Enormous trees—the biggest I'd ever seen. I dusted off my filthy skirt and walked toward them.

Up close, they were almost too massive to be believed. I'd never seen redwoods before, but these must have been similar—enormous and imposing, like a tribe of giants. One had a trunk so thick, six or seven Drake Rosemont students could have stood in a circle, hand in hand, and still not have reached around. The tree's massive roots poked up from the jungle floor and lay like long, sinuous snakes. I ran my hand against the rough bark of the trunk. I'd always liked trees: how they lived so long, how their roots sank deep into the ground, stabilizing them, giving them strength. I rested my head against the trunk. Soon, drops of rain began to fall. I was grateful for those drops, because the mosquitoes finally left me alone. I was grateful until the drops turned into a crashing wave of water, the weight of it shocking and scary. Even under the branches of the giant tree, I was pounded. Droplets as big as robins' eggs pelted my skin. I'd never felt so vulnerable and alone.

Minutes passed—long, drenching minutes. I must have cried, but my tears meant nothing. The rain washed them away as soon as they appeared. I began to go numb again. Maybe that was better. Better to believe this wasn't happening.

When I saw her, I didn't believe it at first. I thought I was hallucinating. It would have been easy to conjure things through the blur of water. But the longer I stared, the more certain I was that she was real. Her Drake Rosemont blouse was untucked as usual. Her lank blond hair hung soggily down her back. Her stiff, awkward stance was instantly recognizable.

I ran, screaming her name. When I reached her, I grabbed on for dear life. Mel let out a wild screech and wrapped me in her arms, squeezing me hard. We both cried out in relief.

"Are you all right?" she demanded.

"I don't know. I think so . . ."

I detached myself long enough to catch a glimpse of gashes on her legs and a deep, bloody gouge on her chin. I touched it gently.

"Thank god you're alive, Sam," she said. Even now, under dire circumstances, her tone was the same: clipped and monotone. People always assumed she was cold or unfeeling. They were wrong.

"Have you seen the others?" I asked.

"No one. You're the first."

Filled with relief, I gave her another hug. Seeing Mel meant recovering hope. She'd take charge. She'd get us through this—somehow.

We huddled under a tree and waited out the sheets of water that fell one after another. At last, the downpour subsided. Mel got down to business immediately. She was still wearing her backpack, and showed me what it contained—some books and notepads. But no technology. No phone. As we double-checked zippered pockets, she told me what she remembered of the flight: After the layover in Honolulu, the pilot had said we would have to stop again. He'd called it "a precautionary measure."

"We were all there when we boarded again—you, me, Rittika and Rish, Jeremiah, Chester, Ming, Avery, Warren, Betty, Anne Marie . . ." she said.

"And Pablo," I added.

"Yeah, Pablo was there. The pilot said everything was all right, that there was no mechanical problem."

"Well, obviously there was."

Mel bit down on her lip. Her lips were always chapped. The Sharpe sisters didn't believe in ChapStick, or any beauty supplies, for that matter.

"I wonder if Coach Coifman knows yet," she mused.

"I still can't believe she wasn't on the plane."

"Me neither."

"And Mr. Singh—I would have thought he would've come."

Rish and Rittika's father, Mr. Singh, was the sponsor of our teams, that is, Drake Rosemont's boys' and girls' fencing teams. He paid for everything: our equipment, uniforms, and travel expenses. We'd come to expect extravagance from Mr. Singh— he was a billionaire, after all—but he'd outdone himself this time. Normally, we flew coach, but for this tournament in Japan, he'd offered our teams the use of his private jet and his own personal pilot. It had been unbelievable, like a dream, that sleek silver jet with leather seats that reclined into beds. Before Drake Rosemont, I'd never even been on a plane. And now I was traveling like a celebrity.

We'd flown out of Logan International Airport in Boston, about an hour from Drake Rosemont. Our final destination was Haneda Airport in Tokyo. Coach Coifman was supposed to be traveling with us, but a sudden family emergency meant she'd arrive twenty-four hours after we landed. Everyone thought our headmaster would cancel the trip—or at least reschedule the flight so that we'd have an adult chaperone. But he'd surprised us by giving the green light.

"I'm letting you go under one condition," he'd told us. "I expect you to be on your best behavior, like the responsible young men and women that I know you are."

I bet that right about now, he regretted his decision.

"Do you think the pilot made it?" Mel asked me.

"I don't know. But I don't have a good feeling."

"Why?"

"You remember how you thought one of his eyes was fake?"

"Yeah?"

"It was."

I took her hand and rolled the eyeball into her palm, then watched her eyes widen, the colorless fans of her lashes spread far apart.

"It's cool," she said, turning it over. "My dad has a collection of prosthetic eyes. Did I ever show them to you?

"No."

"I used to hide them in my sisters' breakfast cereal."

"You're such a freak."

"Yeah, tell me about it."

Thinking about how the eye had felt—wet and sticky in my fingers, I vomited again. It was bile this time; there was nothing left in my stomach to purge. Mel wiped my mouth with her own sleeve. Then she held up the eye for a better look.

"Do you want it back?" she asked.

When I shook my head, she tucked it into one of her knee socks, out of sight.

"Come on," Mel said, "we've got to look for the others." I trudged behind her, willing my feet to move, one after the other. "I saw some wreckage a ways back," she remarked. "I don't know what we'll find, Sam." She didn't sound optimistic, but her jaw was stiff and her expression determined. I'd seen that look a thousand times.

"Which way?" I asked. I wondered if, deep inside, Mel felt as stricken as I did. I wondered if she knew that the only thing keeping me from going crazy was her.

She charged ahead.

The day grew hotter, even under the shade of the canopy. I continued to wipe away sweat, as well as fresh blood on my shins. I rolled up my sleeves to my elbows, baiting the mosquitoes. We walked a long time, until something caught Mel's attention in the distance. I looked in the direction she was staring. There seemed to be a black cloud hovering above the ground. It turned out to be a swarm of flies, dark as a clot. I stopped in my tracks, realizing what they were fussing over. But Mel didn't hesitate to get closer. She actually touched it: a leg. A man's leg. My eyes traveled from the long, narrow foot up a sinewy brown calf dotted with curly black hairs. Above the knee was a mangled stump of flesh. The femur jutted out along with bloody globs of muscle and tissue.

Names trundled through my head—Chester, Pablo, Warren, Rish? It was a good thing I had nothing left to throw up.

"The pilot," Mel said, answering the unasked question.

"You sure?"

"Positive. Look at the knee. That's an old hinge. It couldn't be from one of the boys."

I didn't look again. I'd take her word for it.

Silently, Mel collected a bunch of leaves. She covered the leg until it was invisible on the forest floor.

"That's two missing body parts," she said. "His odds are officially terrible." She must have seen that I was completely losing it, because she added, "But we're okay. We're gonna be okay."

We continued our search, eyes peeled for the dead as well as the living. Meanwhile, the sun continued its scorching arc across the sky, shedding heat and sending bright, slivered rays through the canopy. I was so thirsty I thought I might faint. It was impossible not to think about water while walking through the jungle. The ground was moist. Droplets dripped off the ends of reeds and puddled in the center of leaves. A thick mist clung to the air. Water was everywhere, and yet there was barely enough in any one place to moisten the tongue.

As if reading my mind, Mel stopped in front of an odd-looking shrub. "Here, you can drink from these." She gestured at the reddish orbs that dangled from its branches. They resembled vials and had fluid inside.

I looked at her skeptically.

"It's a pitcher plant," she continued, touching one of the orbs. "My mother has them in her greenhouse."

Mrs. Sharpe was a botanist and a walking, talking encyclopedia of plant-related know-how. Her greenhouse was nearly as large and cluttered as the Sharpe home. It was filled to the brim with trees, flowers, herbs, and stranger things: cactuses, funguses, even algae. With these, Mel's mother made potions, lotions, and medicines, which she sold online. There were so many extraordinary things in her greenhouse, I doubted I'd have remembered the pitcher plants even if I'd seen them before.

"The liquid inside lures insects," Mel explained. "They fall in, and the plant digests them."

I looked at her skeptically. "And this is safe to drink?"

Instead of answering, she squatted and tilted an orb toward her mouth. The liquid poured between her lips. That was enough for me; I was too thirsty for doubt. I followed her lead, drinking orb after orb.

"I want more," I told her.

"I've seen some palms around. We can drink coconut water if we have to. Come on!"

She pulled my arm and we kept moving, slapping mosquitoes, pushing brush and bracken out of our way. I started to walk behind her, following in her footsteps. My ears buzzed with the incessant din of the jungle: droning insects, flapping wings, manic birdsong. Suddenly, a new sound cut through the noise: a female voice. Rittika's. Mel and I looked at each other in astonishment. We'd never been so happy to hear Rittika before. At Drake Rosemont, we usually went out of our way to avoid her.

But she sounded distressed. Her voice, usually haughty and confident, quavered.

We began to run in her direction. As we drew closer, we heard other voices, too—Betty's, and Ming's, and was that Anne Marie's? Suddenly, there was reason to celebrate. Mel and I weren't the only survivors. Some of our teammates—our friends—had made it, too.

We ran faster, till my lungs ached. But it seemed we didn't make it in time.

"If Rish is dead, I might as well be, too!" Rittika declared.

Then I heard a sharp splash and even louder screams.

TWO

THE TANGLE THINNED RIGHT BEFORE WE REACHED

them. Trees and snarled vines gave way to slim palm saplings, stalks of bamboo, and banks of dark moss littered with coconut shells. Though Rittika's words still echoed through my brain, filling me with dread, I was awed by what lay ahead—a huge turquoise lake. An oasis in the middle of the jungle.

Ming, Betty, Anne Marie, and Avery were standing on the shore, oblivious to our presence. They were gazing at something on the far side of the lake. A waterfall.

"What's happening?" Mel yelled.

"Mel, Sam! She jumped! Rittika . . ." Betty's voice began to sputter.

It became instantly clear that Rittika had leapt from the high rock outcrop over which the water flowed. Mel began sprinting toward the waterfall. I followed with the others. We scanned the water as we went, anxious for Rittika to surface, knowing that every second counted. My relief at seeing my friends was quickly fading into fear.

When we'd made it three-quarters of the way, she bobbed up, finally. My heart stopped racing a million miles a minute. I was almost as grateful to see her as I'd been to see Mel.

"Why did you do that?" Avery screamed in her nasal voice. Kicking off her shoes, she jumped into the lake and swam toward Rittika. She was a good swimmer; we all were. Everyone enrolled at Drake Rosemont took swimming lessons in the Olympic-size pool named after some rich alum. Mastery of the breaststroke, backstroke, and butterfly were required for graduation. You always knew who had been in the pool by the chlorine stink of their hair.

"I wish I'd drowned," Rittika exclaimed petulantly. Her long black hair was a shiny oil slick down her back.

"Don't say that!" Ming called from the pebbly shore.

"I mean it."

Avery reached Rittika, grabbed her hand, and began to tow her back to shore. She'd learned the technique in swim rescue class, which was also mandatory at Drake Rosemont. Rittika allowed herself to be pulled. She made minimal effort to move, kicking her feet casually.

When the girls reached the shore, we pulled them up. Rittika wrapped her arms around herself and shivered, despite the heat. She was wearing nothing but her underwear: a pink bra and panties. On some nearby rocks I caught sight of her school uniform: Drake Rosemont's official gray-and-maroon plaid, a white blouse, and knee socks. Her oxfords—the ones we all wore grudgingly—lay on the ground. For the first time since starting private school, I was grateful for those shoes, for their thick soles and sturdy steel shanks. I doubted sneakers would have gotten me through the muddy jungle.

"You scared the hell out of us," Avery said, still trying to catch her breath. She was a square-shaped girl whose sorry looks were more obvious because she always hung around Rittika, who was beautiful.

"I told you—if we don't find Rish, that's it for me. I'm done," Rittika replied. Rish was her twin brother, and the two of them were inseparable at Drake Rosemont.

Avery sighed and began to wring water from her skirt. I could tell she didn't know what to say, that she was as scared and uncertain as everyone else.

In silence, we stared at the waterfall, at the foamy white splash and the churning water below it. If I squinted, I could see water funneling like a miniature tornado underneath the surface. Around the perimeter of the plunge pool, the water was darker. Navy rather than aqua, dark and dim with silt. I wondered how deep it was.

Suddenly, I felt someone hug me from behind. Betty. Now that Rittika's emergency was over, the other girls told Mel and me how happy they were to see us. Even Anne Marie, easily the shyest of the group, squeezed my hand. There was an outpouring of affection and concern. Wringing hands touched various injuries. Ming had a huge lump on her skull, above her right ear. Avery said she felt like she'd eaten glass. Betty's wound was the worst of the bunch. She had a deep, blood-soaked laceration near her elbow—easily cause for a trip to the emergency room. But I doubted we were anywhere near a hospital.

Mel ripped off the hem of her skirt. She took Betty's arm and began to bandage her oozing wound. As she did so, Rittika noticed Mel's chin, which had finally stopped bleeding.

"I hope that doesn't scar," Rittika remarked. I wasn't sure if she was being sincere or sarcastic. But I did know the comment was the first thing she'd said to Mel in months. Usually, Rittika ignored Mel. Most of the girls at school did. There were many reasons for Mel's lack of popularity. For one thing, she was socially awkward—physically, too. And for another, she was smarter than everyone else. That tended to put people off. Mel was first in our class in almost every subject. Our school could have dedicated a whole showcase to the trophies, plaques, and ribbons she'd won in Math League competitions, spelling bees, chess club championships, and quiz bowls. But the more recognition she got, the more the other girls mocked her. Behind her back, they laughed at her wide hips and loping stride. They laughed at the fact that Amelia Earhart was not only her namesake but also her idol.

Maybe Mel was destined to be obsessed with the lost flier. Maybe that's what happens when you're linked to someone from the second you're born. From the time she could read, she'd devoured every piece of information she could get on Earhart. Mel even dressed like her sometimes, in a brown leather skullcap, white flying scarf, and knee-high boots. She got away with wearing these things, which were strictly against the dress code, because she'd written a book about Earhart: a seven-hundred-page biography published to great acclaim. It won literary prizes and was translated into five languages. Mel even got royalty checks for it. Not bad for a teenager. Not bad for Drake Rosemont's reputation either.

But the downside to her success was that it set her apart. Far apart. The girls were jealous, the boys cowed. Even our teachers treated her differently. Only her family and I continued to talk to her like she was a regular person.

And yet, right now, I knew our classmates were relieved to see her. For if anyone could help us, it was Mel.

"How did you find this place?" I asked. "Where are the boys? Where are we?" The questions came out in a sputtering pile.

"Anne Marie and I crashed down over there," Betty said, pointing somewhere beyond the outcrop of the waterfall. "The others found their way here when they heard our voices."

"They carry," Mel said. "The boulders around the lake form a natural echo chamber."

Rittika looked at her askance.

"Where are the boys?" I repeated.

"Have you seen my brother?" Rittika asked, buttoning her blouse.

"No."

"We have no clue about any of the boys except Jeremiah," Betty said.

"Where is he?" I asked.

Betty put her hand on my arm. I trained my eyes on her

wound—realizing that what she had to say might be just as dreadful.

"Avery saw him. She found him in the jungle. Dead."

"Oh my god."

Rittika exhaled and for about half a second her pissy-haughty veneer, the spoiled rich girl role she played so well, disintegrated. I was sure she was thinking about Rish, praying that his fate was different.

"Can you bring us to him?" Mel asked Avery.

"Why would you ask me to do that? You heard her—he's dead!"

"He might have something on him we can use—a cell, some means of news or communication."

"Is she serious?" Avery asked, looking at me.

People always wanted me to decode Mel. They thought I was her translator. In truth, I was—and not just hers. When my father invited his Indian relatives over—uncles, aunties, and cousins who stayed in the spare bedroom, attic, and even my room—my mother expected me to decipher their needs. She'd shove me in front of her when she asked them if they wanted tea.

"*Chai?*" I'd ask.

"*Acha,*" they'd respond, waggling their heads from side to side, which my mother knew meant "yes," not "no," but still she'd pull me into the kitchen with her, peppering me with questions. As if I should know the answers. As if by virtue of my half-Indianness, I could figure out their needs.

"She's serious," I confirmed.

"Okay, fine," Avery said with a sigh.

Her hands in knots, Avery led the way. Jeremiah's body wasn't far from the lake, but it was still hard to find through the sea of green. A million mosquito bites later, we arrived at a patch of jungle that looked pretty much like everywhere else.

"He was here. I swear he was here," Avery said.

"I see him," Mel replied, pointing.

We gasped when we saw Jeremiah's body, or what had been his body. Now it was more or less a mangled heap of flesh and bloodied clothing jammed between a tree trunk and a cluster of bushes. One by one, we looked away, queasy, repelled, more afraid than ever. I stared at the ground near my feet, but saw something just as disturbing: a trail of blood that had trickled from the dark red pool that surrounded his body all the way to my shoes. Marching on that trail were insects: many-legged centipede-like things that made my skin crawl. They seemed to be eating Jeremiah's blood, feasting on it. By comparison, the mosquitoes now looked like saints.

Mel walked up to the body. She didn't bat an eye as she untangled his limbs and searched his clothes. Coming up empty, she inspected the ground all around him, the bushes and saplings and vines.

"Nothing," she said.

"Should we bury him?" Betty asked.

"Not now. Let's concentrate on the ones who are alive."

I watched Anne Marie take a couple of steps back and vomit.

Mel threw a bunch of leaves and branches over Jeremiah as she'd done with the pilot's leg. Then she looked up. I knew she was trying to find the position of the sun, although it was almost impossible to see through the leafy canopy.

"It'll get dark soon," she said. "We should go back to the lake. Find something to drink, get our strength up."

"No way," Rittika replied. "I'm going to keep looking for my brother."

"I don't think that's a good idea."

"What do you know?"

"I think she means that it's better if we stay in one place," I interjected. "Remember when you were little and your mother said, 'If you get lost, stay put'? It's the same situation here. Rish stands a better chance of finding you if you stop moving."

"Unless he can't walk," Rittika pointed out. I caught a trace of a British accent. It came out from time to time. Prim and proper, it made her sound even more like a snob. I'd never admit it, but I'd tried to imitate it once or twice.

"No one will be able to find anyone once it's dark," Mel said.

Rittika glared at her, but finally agreed to return with us to the lake. When we got there, the water seemed different. More translucent. Or maybe it was just that I was taking the time to really look at it. Except for the churning water of the plunge pool, the lake was clear. I could make out a school of electric-blue fish swimming near the surface. Closer to the bottom, long needle-shaped fish darted to and fro. I saw the scuttle of a crab and the undulation of sea plants. Along the periphery of the lake, I admired pinkish boulders and graceful, bending palms. It was a beautiful place—too bad it had taken a disaster to find it.

I sat down on a slim crescent of beach. The pebbly sand warm against my bare legs, I tried to relax, taking deep breaths. But I was soon startled by more screaming.

"Avery, what are you doing?" Ming screeched. I saw that Avery was standing on the lip of the outcrop, thick arms flailing. She looked like a nervous tightrope walker.

"Getting something for Rittika," she called out. She took a sloppy leap into the water, landing feetfirst. I jumped up, sure we'd lost another classmate. I scanned the whirlpool, but didn't see her inside. The dark water seemed to have swallowed her whole.

Just as Mel was about to dive in and look for her, Avery came up, hands first. She was holding something large and pale and pointed. Relieved, the girls and I watched her swim ashore. We circled her as she clambered sloppily onto a mossy bank.

"I—I got it," she said triumphantly, her cheeks ruddy from exertion. She was in her underwear, as Rittika had been. The elastic waistband of her panties cut into the pale bloat of her belly.

"What is that?" Betty asked. Avery held it up—a shell: radiant, pink white, dominated by a spiky spire. About eight inches in diameter, it was flawless, without a single chip or barnacle.

Avery handed it to Rittika and we gathered closer, the shell our gleaming nucleus. We watched her turn it over and run her fingers over the lip, which was thin and scalloped. Inside, the shell was pink, dark as our tongues. Dripping water, the mouth looked shiny and smooth, wide and deep. Rittika's whole hand fit inside as she removed sand and bits of seagrass.

"It's a conch," Mel said.

"I thought I spotted something down there," said Rittika.

"There are more, too," added Avery.

"My father has one in his shell collection," Mel said. She reached out to take the shell, but Rittika held it fast. "It's much smaller than this one and not as nice. His is a queen conch. Maybe this is one, too. Or maybe it's something else—something new."

Her eyes sparkled at the possibility.

"Is it valuable?" Rittika asked.

I wasn't surprised by the question. Rittika talked about money like other people discuss the weather. That is, often. She liked to brag that her family owned at least one mansion on every continent. While the rest of us slummed it in jeans and sweats on the weekends, she wore haute couture. Sometimes she took Avery and Ming on shopping sprees in Boston, armed with her father's AmEx black card. She boasted that he was the richest man in India, and that she and Rish would inherit his company one day.

"Valuable? It depends what you mean," Mel replied. "It has practical value, sure. The shell is used to make tools and jewelry, and the animal that lives inside is edible. But this one's hollow. Whoever lived there's gone."

I couldn't explain why, but there was something

mesmerizing about the conch—its spiral tip, especially. It seemed to wind on and on, infinitely. It reminded me of time and space, things that have no beginning or end. Judging by their expressions, I could see the other girls were just as riveted.

"How many more conchs are down there?" Mel asked Avery.

"Dozens and dozens."

"Good. We can retrieve them—the ones with meat. That way we won't have to live on coconuts."

"What do you mean 'live on'?" Rittika asked, her eyebrow raised.

"She just means it's a good thing you found food," I said hastily. "In case we get hungry."

Still holding fast to the conch, Rittika laughed nervously. "So we're to eat your cousins, eh?" she asked the shell, staring into its mouth. Her lips curved into a sly smile.

"What?" Ming demanded.

"I knew it reminded me of something! Here, look inside. See how it's smooth and moist? Don't you think there's something *feminine* about it?"

Ming looked confusedly into the shell's mouth.

"I'll give you a hint," Rittika said. "Think about how you spell 'conch.' Now change the 'n' to an 'o' . . ."

Avery chortled. Betty cracked a smile. But Ming just turned red.

"Don't be disgusting," she whined.

"Don't be a prude," Rittika retorted.

Ming cringed. In the hierarchy of Rittika's friends, she was firmly in second place, lagging behind Avery. It was no wonder. She was like a wet dish towel—totally lacking in personality. In fact, whenever someone referred to her, it was always in relation to Rittika, as if she had no identity of her own. Ming was Rittika's friend, Rittika's sidekick, Rittika's minion.

"Do you want to hold it?" Rittika asked me.

I was surprised when she passed the conch to me. She didn't usually pay me much attention.

Gingerly, I examined the shell. The inside really did look like a girl's privates, exposed. But I wasn't embarrassed, not like Ming. Sex and bodies were topics of endless curiosity and discussion at Drake Rosemont. Some of us spoke from experience, like Rittika. Others—like myself or Betty—from a theoretical perspective. The witching hour was usually 11:00 p.m., when most of us couldn't stand looking at our homework a second longer but didn't want to sleep, either. We would wander toward the room with the most voices. We sought knowledge, and often got it, whether it be an impromptu talk on how to get a boy to like you, or directions on how to hook up. More often than not, it was Rittika who gave us tips.

Those late-night discussions were some of my favorite times at Drake Rosemont. I loved the secret sharing, the bonding. I loved that at any moment a juicy bit of gossip might be revealed, and that that gossip could touch any of our lives, even mine. The boys who so fascinated us were tantalizingly close. Their dormitory was only a five-minute stroll away. All of us—guys and girls—took the same classes, had the same professors, and ate in the same dining hall. We even, in some cases, played the same sports. There was a reason I had started fencing—I wanted to hang around with the boys' team. And yet for all that overlap, boys were still a mystery to me. I never had the sense of familiarity, of easy intimacy, with them that I had with girls, especially Mel and her sisters.

Sometimes I wondered if the boys were as curious about us as we were about them. After curfew, did they gaze at our building, watching the lights in our windows and thinking that our brick dormitory was a fortress of secrets?

I suspected they did.

And now? Where were the boys? Were the survivors as confused and terrified as we were? *Were* there survivors? All the girls had made it through the crash, bruised, battered, and bloody, but luckily—miraculously—alive. But the boys had already lost one of their own, and maybe more.

After Rittika's joke, a gloom set in. Despite wanting to cling to the conch, my first instinct was to pass it to Mel. She, in turn, gave it to Anne Marie. Hand to hand, the shell traveled in a silent circle. When it came back to me, I had a premonition. I sensed that new rules were being written, right then and there, rules much harsher than those at Drake Rosemont. But I couldn't yet say what they were.

THREE

MEL TICKED OFF ON HER FINGERS WHAT WE NEEDED
to do. One, find water. Two, find food. Three, take shelter. Four, build a fire. Five, ensure our safety. One, two, three, four, five. The steps of survival. If only it were that easy.

"The boys don't even make your list," Rittika hissed.

"If we build a big fire, everyone within a mile will be able to see it. Rish included," Mel replied.

Mel enlisted me and Anne Marie to help her. We spread out and collected pieces of kindling and pats of brown moss—anything that counted as tinder. Mel tore a few pages from a notebook in her backpack and crumpled them into wads. With these items she built a small pyramid in a crevice between two boulders. Scouring the area, she found two pinkish stones, which she proceeded to bang together above the pyramid. Soon there was a spark, followed by a tiny glow atop the peak. Mel waved her hand above it and blew at it gently. Gradually, it transformed into a plume of smoke, then a lick of fire.

I was impressed, but not surprised. Mel was the most self-reliant person I knew. Or maybe the second-most. First place would have to go to her father, Amis Sharpe. He could survive anywhere, from the African savanna to the Arctic Circle.

Mr. Sharpe was as impressive as Mel's mother. He called himself a naturalist, but what he really was was an adventurer. A man obsessed with desert, ocean, mountain, and valley. A man determined to see as much of this world as he possibly could before he died. I'm sure he spent at least half of every year jumping from shore to shore. He favored those places hard to access and little traveled. He didn't like the idea of following in someone else's footsteps.

So great was Mr. Sharpe's love of adventure that he'd named Mel and her older sisters after famous explorers: Drake for Sir Francis Drake, who led an expedition around the world; Gaspar for Gaspar Corte-Real, the Portuguese navigator who sailed to Greenland; Tasman for Abel Tasman, discoverer of New Zealand; and Leif, for Leif Erikson, the first European to land in North America. Mel was the only Sharpe daughter named after a woman: Amelia Earhart, the famous aviatrix. Her father, the fifth time around, had shown some restraint and given his youngest a prettier, more conventional name.

The funny thing was my friend never went by "Amelia," though she loved her namesake. She preferred "Mel." She said it was just easier to say. Me—I think she wanted to be like her sisters, who had been named after guys.

I dropped a pile of kindling beside the fire. Fanning the flames with a palm frond, Mel told me to get more. "Everything you can find," she said.

I obliged, passing Betty and Ming as I looked around. They were busy cracking coconut shells against some boulders that shouldered the lake. Betty motioned for me to come over. She gave me a sip of warm, sweet water straight from the shell. It tasted like heaven.

"Every coconut has only a little bit of water, but we'll get what we can," Betty said determinedly.

Making my way around the lake, I watched Avery and Rittika dive for more conch shells. Mel had told them to find ones with meat. They obeyed, I think, because they wanted to be in the water. Normally, Rittika would never follow Mel's orders.

As the sun began to sink, everybody returned to the fire. Rittika and Avery carried five shells—they claimed they all had meat.

"Nice!" Mel told them.

"There are a lot down below the waterfall," Avery replied.

"I think that's the deepest part of conch lake," Rittika added.

The name—Conch Lake—instantly stuck. Probably because it was Rittika who said it. She was always starting trends. Even now, we were all wearing the same chipped nail polish we'd seen her wear a month ago. Orange Crush, it was called.

Avery licked her lips. "God, I'm thirsty," she complained. "The water's so salty."

"You drank out of Conch Lake?" Mel asked, her eyes widening.

"Just a little."

"How much?"

"Like a soda can's worth?"

"You stupid, stupid girl!"

Appalled, Avery stared at her.

"Salt water relieves your thirst only at first," Mel explained. "But then you have to pee to get rid of all the extra sodium. You'll be dehydrated soon, if you aren't already."

"So what do I do?" Avery demanded. Her hands were in knots again.

"To start, stop drinking from Conch Lake."

"I get that. But what do I do about what I've already drunk? Am I—am I going to . . ."

"Get sick? Die?" Mel let the questions linger in the air. "Probably not," she conceded.

"So what do I *do*?"

Mel looked at her in exasperation. "Have a seat," she said, pointing to a boulder. "Maybe you'll learn something."

Avery did as told. Then Mel aligned the five conch shells in a row. "You have to be firm about it," she said, picking up the first one in line. "The conch has a strong hold on its home. It uses a muscle with suction power. To get the meat out, you have two choices: smash the shell or break the seal."

Rittika took a seat next to Avery. She picked up a conch and touched the shiny-slick animal that poked out of the mouth. It retracted immediately. Her finger retracted with equal speed.

"That's just gross," she said.

"It's a mollusk," Mel said matter-of-factly.

She took a second shell and banged its sharp tip into the

spiral of the first. After a few direct hits, and a couple of way-ward ones, she made a hole.

"Okay, that should do it."

She proceeded to dredge out the meat with a thin stick. Free from its shell, it looked pretty disgusting. I'd been hoping for something like a supermarket chicken breast: pale pink and clean-scrubbed. This, by contrast, reminded me of the pig's heart that our biology teacher kept in a jar of formaldehyde on his desk.

Mel pointed out the mud-brown "foot" that the conch had used to creep along the bottom of Conch Lake. She showed us the thick, rubbery outer skin and the digestive system with its blue-purple membrane. Each part was less appetizing than the last. She then laid the conch meat on a boulder and attacked it with a round stone.

"What the hell are you doing?" Rittika demanded.

"I'm simultaneously killing it and tenderizing it," she replied, nonplussed.

Rittika and Avery stared at each other in dismay.

When Mel was through, she washed the meat in the lake, poked two sticks through it, and told me to hold it over the fire. I did what she asked without question. In truth, a part of me felt like I was in the middle of a dream, that none of this was quite real. I guess I was still in shock.

I turned the makeshift kebabs as Betty stoked the fire. Both of us watched Mel retrieve and clean the rest of the meat. She put these on skewers, too. When Betty offered to cook them, Mel took off her socks and shoes and headed for Conch Lake. I wondered why—I doubted she'd find more shells now. It was getting dark. From a distance I watched her lean over and drink water from cupped hands.

"Didn't she just yell at Avery for doing that?" I said.

Betty nodded and shrugged.

Mel proceeded to move around the lake, drinking water from several different places. Then she made her way to the outcrop. I could tell from the way she moved—slowly and cautiously—that the outcrop was slippery.

At the top, she wobbled, then knelt. Cupping her hands again, she drank once more. What was going through her mind? I wondered. It was anyone's guess. Finally, she returned to the fire. She looked at the browning conch, which was beginning to smell good, despite how it looked.

"How much longer?" I asked.

"A few more minutes."

"What about those?" I asked her, nodding to the sticks. They were charred and ashy.

"They should hold up. Don't let the meat fall into the fire. If you can do that, we'll not only have dinner, but plenty of drinking water."

"Are you kidding me?"

She shook her head.

"But I thought Conch Lake was salty," I said.

"It's brackish—part salt, part fresh. The ocean is reaching it. I don't know how—maybe through underground springs. But the waterfall's coming from a different source. That source is nonsaline."

"Nonsaline? You mean drinkable?"

"Yup."

I smiled widely, feeling glad for the first time since the crash. I handed the brittle sticks to Mel before she could object. Kicking off my shoes and socks, tugging off my blouse and skirt, I made a run for the outcrop.

"Hey!" she yelled in my wake, but I didn't turn back.

I'd been right about the outcrop being slippery. I nearly fell as I climbed up. Slimy algae covered many of the boulders. The rocks wobbled underfoot. One actually rolled right out from under me, careening loudly down the bluff and into the water. The splash suddenly made me the center of attention. I scrambled up the last few rocks awkwardly, conscious of my scrawny butt, padded bra, and the big discolored patch on my shoulder—a birthmark I'd always been embarrassed about. It wasn't like me to showcase my body. In fact, the words *showcase* and *my body* didn't even belong in the same sentence. Flushed with embarrassment, I teetered on the outcrop. I was pretty sure I'd meet the same fate as that tumbling rock.

Ever so carefully, ever so slowly, I knelt. I cupped my hands as Mel had. With my back hunched, I took a sip of water. Clean, good, safe, lifesaving. After that first taste, I forgot that the girls were staring. I didn't care how stupid I looked. All I cared about was getting more water into my body. I gulped and gulped. I must have drunk a gallon's worth.

The girls, realizing what was happening, ran over to the waterfall. The coconut water had barely made a dent. Their tongues were still parched. Back on the ground, I told them about Mel's find. Quickly, they formed a human chain up the boulders, holding hands so that no one would slip. It was a beautiful display of collaboration, but it made me uneasy somehow. Maybe I was still thinking about that premonition.

When I came back to Mel, the sun was almost gone, and the horizon was white-hot and ringed with lavender. Mel had just finished cooking the rest of the conchs. They lay on a palm frond.

"Go ahead, Rockwell. You must be starving," she said.

I cringed a little at the sound of my nickname. "Don't you want the first bite?"

"Who said I didn't take it?"

Cautiously, I sampled a piece of conch. To my surprise, it was delicious: smoky and tender, chewy but not tough. I couldn't remember the last time I'd eaten. I took a bite, then another. I had to restrain myself from eating more. There were seven of us girls; I couldn't be greedy.

Mel called the others. They arrived in seconds, propelled by hunger and the mouthwatering smell. I watched with amusement as they devoured the meat. At Drake Rosemont, we were expected to eat like ladies. Entering students had to take a seminar on dining etiquette: how to cut meat correctly, which fork to use for which course, even which topics constituted passable mealtime conversation. It was entertaining to watch my classmates forget everything they'd learned. They licked their fingers and ripped the fibrous meat apart with their teeth. When Avery spit out a piece of shell, all I could think of was Miss Peck, the etiquette teacher. She would've fainted.

All too soon, the conchs were gone. Rittika declared she was still hungry—and she wasn't alone.

"I'm going to look in the jungle," she said. "I remember seeing banana trees."

"But it's dark now," warned Avery.

"There's still a little light. I'll be fine."

"I don't advise it," said Mel. "Why don't you eat some coconut meat? We have plenty of that."

Rittika looked at her contemptuously. "Who died and made you my mother?"

With a flip of her hair, she vanished into the jungle. Ming and Avery looked at each other, then ran after her.

I whispered to Mel that it wasn't a bad idea—to look for fruit.

"I didn't say it was," she said with a sigh. "It's just that—we might be in danger here. Wherever here is."

I knew what she meant. The jungle looked much more

ominous now that darkness was falling. Everything lay in shadows. Still, it was hard to ignore my rumbling stomach.

"Can't I look right around Conch Lake?" I asked her.

She shrugged. "It's up to you."

Betty joined me in foraging the jungle in an area behind the outcrop. It didn't take long before Anne Marie came, too. To our surprise, we spotted not only bananas but wild mangoes. We took as many as we could and trekked back to the fire. We ate the bananas quickly, but the mangoes were tough to peel. In the end, we smashed them against the rocks to split their tough skins. The fruit inside was tart, but I dug in anyway. Pulp ringing my mouth, juice running down my chin, I thought again of Miss Peck.

The others returned soon after. They, too, had found bananas. Our stomachs finally full, we felt revived. For a time we sat around the fire, adding sticks and leaves, and watching smoke drift steadily into the air until it blended into the night sky. Though we didn't speak much, I knew we were all thinking about the boys. I wondered if they would ever find us—if they *could* find us.

I was glad when Mel whistled suddenly. Glad to have something to focus on other than worry. She stood up and held the conch over her head. By the light of the fire, it gleamed, demanding our attention.

"I know you're tired," she said, "but there are things we need to do."

"Like rest," Avery complained. "I feel like my body's falling apart."

"We're all bruised and sore," Mel replied. "But we can't focus on ourselves. We still have to maintain the fire. Not to mention keep a lookout for the boys, rescuers, maybe even intruders. We should take turns. Then everyone will have a chance to sleep."

I nodded but could see that Mel's speech hadn't motivated everyone. Avery lay down beside the fire and shut her eyes. Rittika sulked. The words *have to* and *should* didn't apply to her. She might very well have been thinking about ways to find her brother, but the decision to act wouldn't come from Mel.

"Does anyone know what time it is?" Ming asked absently.

"This says three, but I think it's broken," Anne Marie said. She was glancing at a gold watch she liked to wear. She'd told me once it had been her great-grandfather's. As she held it to her ear, she looked ready to cry. "It stopped ticking," she whispered.

"Who will take a turn?" Mel asked, running her finger around the spiral of the conch.

"I will," I said.

"So will I," Betty added, after a beat.

Sniffing a little, Anne Marie agreed, too.

Mel waited, staring at the other three girls, the ones who hadn't answered. They ignored her. Looking back at Mel, I saw that her face was red. I figured she was steaming mad at the girls who refused to participate, but then I realized she was sun-burned. Badly sunburned. A great pink banner waved across her pale forehead. The apples of her cheeks were on fire. I felt my own cheeks, relieved that they felt cool to the touch.

"So it's the four of us, then," she said softly, looking at Betty, Anne Marie, and me. She tilted her head and stared at the sky above Conch Lake. "At least it's a clear night. A plane might be able to spot our fire."

A ripple of hope went through me. After seeing Jeremiah's body and the pilot's eye and leg, I needed something positive to cling to. "You think they're already looking for us?"

"Definitely. I'm guessing we're big news back home. Think about it: a bunch of private school kids missing after a plane crash? The networks will be all over it. And don't forget how famous Mr. Singh is. His name alone will make headlines."

"Maybe no one knows we're missing yet."

"Don't be silly. Of course they do."

"How do you know?"

Mel looked at me as if I'd been born yesterday. "Sam, tech-nology for tracking is very sophisticated. Satellites and radar monitor almost everything."

"You said 'almost.'"

"They know we went down," she insisted.

I didn't argue. What did I know about airplanes and radar anyway? Nothing. Mel was probably right. I decided to trust her. Even if I still had a bad feeling, I desperately wanted to believe everything was going to be okay.

"What I'm really concerned about is where we are," she said. "Don't you wonder? Is it a continent or an island? I have no idea, only that it's somewhere in the South Pacific. I should have been paying better attention."

I could understand Mel's sense of bewilderment. It felt bizarre to have no sense of place, of context, almost like we didn't exist at all—or rather, like we'd been reborn somewhere else, somewhere completely new.

"We'll probably find out tomorrow," I said.

"I hope so, Rockwell."

I smiled at her weakly. Mel had started calling me Rockwell years ago, upon meeting my family over a Thanksgiving break. In contrast to her eccentric parents and siblings, she'd found mine as wholesome and all-American as a Norman Rockwell painting. She couldn't get over our collective appearance: my dark, handsome father; my blond mother with her perfectly bobbed hair; my sister, Alexa, who was exceptionally pretty, if frail.

My mother set a simple but inviting Thanksgiving table. She covered our scuffed dining table with an old lace tablecloth, put out our good plates (unmatching, but unchipped), and decorated the place settings with cheerful little baskets of acorns and pinecones she'd collected herself. Thanksgiving was my mother's favorite holiday. She liked the ceremony of it: the presentation of a perfect bird, saying grace, passing each dish around the table in a clockwise direction. Thanksgiving was one of the few days of the year when she wasn't bitter.

Surprisingly, Mel didn't see through the facade. She looked at us and listened to our polite, impersonal conversations and fell for the act. She didn't notice that my mother was a little slow because she was doped up on Xanax. She didn't realize that Alexa moved things around her plate but didn't put anything in her mouth. When my father said that Alexa was home for Thanksgiving break, Mel didn't dig deeper to find out the real story. Alexa was home indefinitely. She'd lost so much weight while at college that she'd passed out a couple of times. The administration told her to take time off and get treatment. She wouldn't be able to restart school midway through the year, so she would be bumped back to the next graduating class.

The college probably thought it was doing Alexa a favor, but the truth was, it was making her situation worse. My parents were ignoring her problem. Alexa told me they thought therapy was expensive and indulgent; what she needed was willpower. So now she was stuck at home, in the middle of the usual family dysfunction, too weak and depressed to fend for herself.

At one point, Alexa took me into her room to hide. That was *our* Thanksgiving tradition: Escape the 'rents as soon as possible, for as long as possible.

"I knew it would be bad to be home," she told me. "But it's even worse than I thought."

"Why?"

"They don't even speak to each other anymore," she confessed. "They're either arguing or silent, one or the other, every day. I wish they had the balls to divorce once and for all."

"You know they never will. They live in their own warped little bubble."

Alexa nodded. "Listen, from now on, I think you should stay away. Find somewhere else to go during school vacations. It's not safe here."

"What do you mean 'not safe'?"

"You know what I mean," she replied pointedly. And I did. I knew our father took his anger out on Alexa, sometimes with words, sometimes leaving bruises and welts on her skin.

Seeing my sister this way, I didn't want to leave her all alone. I offered to drop out of Drake Rosemont and return to my old high school so she'd have an ally, but she shook her head.

"I say this because I love you: You got away, now stay away."

"I don't want to stay away. I want to be with you."

"Don't worry about me."

"Of course I'm going to worry!"

She wrapped her arms around herself—maybe because she was cold (she was always cold), maybe because she needed to comfort herself. "I don't have to stick around here forever, you know. I'm eighteen. I could go anywhere."

"Where would you go?"

That's when she faltered. Her bravado had more holes in it than Swiss cheese.

"Just don't worry," she repeated.

But I did.

That Thanksgiving, Mel didn't know about my conversation with my sister. She was too busy chatting with my father about this and that. He could be charming when he wanted to be—that was his trick. How he fooled people. So she remained ignorant of certain things, the most important things. She didn't even suspect anything when I asked her if I could start staying at her place during breaks. She just figured I preferred the wildness of her house to the formality of mine. Ironically, she clung to the idea that my family was some stereotypical ideal. A Rockwell painting. I knew she meant it as a compliment, but still I was embarrassed. And upset. Though she was my best friend, she had no idea how many skeletons I hid in the closet.

"Did you hear me?" she asked, shaking me into the present. "I'm going to take the first shift—patrolling the area. Betty and Anne Marie said they'd keep an eye on the fire. So you're free to sleep for a while, if you want."

"I think I'll go for a swim," I replied, getting up. "I'm too stressed to sleep."

"Suit yourself."

Though the night had cooled the jungle, Conch Lake was still the temperature of bathwater. It sloshed gently around my face as I floated on my back, kicking my feet, watching stars flicker in the sky. They were much brighter here than they were at home, almost like they were different stars altogether.

Water plugged my ears until I heard nothing but the lake itself: lapping, lulling, alive. I felt shut in. Cradled. I loved the feeling—it reminded me of swim lessons at Drake Rosemont. At the end of our sessions, the instructor usually let us have a few minutes to ourselves. I always looked forward to that time, when I could just float. In the water, I didn't think or worry. It was as if I were suspended above my problems.

The air felt brisk when I emerged and rejoined the other girls. Ming and Avery had given up trying to sleep. Now they were sitting around Rittika, who was standing. She spoke animatedly. All eyes were fixed on her long limbs, caramel skin, and flashbulb-bright teeth. She was like Helen of Troy, the definition of perfect female beauty.

Staring at her, I felt a familiar gnawing of envy and admiration. I wasn't sure which I wanted more, to hate her or be her friend—or maybe both? All I knew for sure was that in the world of teenage girls, Rittika's looks gave her staggering power.

Google revealed that Rittika wasn't the only gorgeous girl in her family. Her mother was a former Miss World. When I looked at old pictures of her on the web, I saw that Mrs. Singh had been every bit as stunning as Rittika was now. It seemed unfair that any family should have such good genes.

I was still studying Rittika when the newcomers arrived. They came from the jungle, drawn by the smoke, our voices, and the moony glow of bare skin, the glisten of Rittika's in particular. From behind the trees came three—tall, broad-shouldered, smelling of moss, musk, blood, and earth. We identified them first by the long shape of their shadows.

"The boys!" Ming screeched.

FOUR

CHESTER, RISH, AND PABLO—THEY HAD SURVIVED.

As soon as I spotted them, I was as giddy as I was relieved. Chester, in particular, always made me feel this way. All I had to do was look at him and I felt completely different: more alert and alive. They were ecstatic upon seeing us, too. Bear hugs all around, and Chester swung a few of us around like rag dolls, me included. I loved the feel of his strong arms around me. Rish and Rittika couldn't stop clinging to each other.

The boys were freaked out, torn up, and thirsty as hell. We took them to the outcrop, where they drank and drank. Chester lay there, belly-down, letting the water slosh around his body. Afterward, we all sat close to the fire and talked. Rish and Chester said they'd crashed near each other, then wandered for hours, calling our names. They'd met Pablo somewhere in the middle of the jungle. Along the way, they also met a little monkey that had started to follow them.

"It was the strangest creature. Totally tame," Rish said, "like someone's pet or something."

"How did you find us?" Mel asked.

"The fire," Pablo said. "Chester saw it first. The closer we got, the more sure I was you guys were hunters or poachers. We had our swords out, just in case!"

Pablo smiled and motioned to Chester's fencing bag—their sole remaining possession from the crash. It had a few blades in it, Chester's mask and uniform, and some peanut shells. The boys—and the monkey—had devoured the nuts hours ago.

Pablo's smile disappeared when we told him about Jeremiah.

"And Warren?" he asked.

"We haven't seen him," Mel said. "We were hoping you had."

"We looked for everybody. But all we found was wreckage."

For the first time, Mel and I told the others about the pilot's missing leg and eye.

Rittika shot me a scornful look. "You could've mentioned that before, Samantha," she said. I shrugged, unwilling to admit that I'd been waiting for Mel to say it first.

"I had a bad feeling about that pilot," Pablo said.

"Why do you say that?" asked Rittika.

"I mean, what kind of pilot has only one good eye?"

She gaped at him. "You didn't have a bad feeling when you got a free flight!"

I sighed, thinking that was a nasty thing to say. Like me, Pablo was at Drake Rosemont on a scholarship. Everyone assumed it was a sports scholarship because he was a good fencer. Either way, the bottom line was the same: Without Mr. Singh's generosity, he wouldn't have been able to afford the trip to Japan. And neither would I.

"Look, I'm not blaming your father for the crash," he said.

"Indirectly, you kind of were," she replied.

"Come on, that's enough," Rish said, putting his hand on his sister's shoulder. "No one's blaming anyone. It was an accident—a terrible accident."

"That's right," agreed Chester. "And it's in the past. We're here now and we have to deal with it."

Rish nodded. "We should go through the wreckage," he said. "See what's there. Maybe there's something useful. A radio or something."

"We should look for Warren," said Pablo.

"I don't think we should do anything right now," replied Mel, looking at the night sky. "Tomorrow, when it's light, we'll search."

"We'll be rescued in the morning," Rittika said confidently. "By now my father must have hundreds of men looking for us."

"Thank god," Avery added.

We talked more about when we might be rescued, how, and by whom. Everyone except Chester, who seemed preoccupied with the fire. He was nervous and restless, intermittently throwing things into the flames: leaves, coconut shells, vines, branches. Most of the girls laughed, but I didn't. We were in enough trouble without his antics. They were okay at fencing practice, but not here.

Suddenly, the fire sprayed sparks—Chester had thrown in a rotting log. Flames darted out in all directions, dangerously close to where we huddled. Most of the girls screeched, pulling back. Mel stood up. Knowing that he had their attention, Chester took off his shirt and beat his chest like Tarzan. Then he picked up Rittika, who laughed, and pretended to toss her in, too. After she playfully slapped him, he put her down.

Soon Rish got in on the act. The two boys circled the fire, daring each other closer to the flames. The shapes of their bodies were exaggerated by the interplay of shadow and light. Rish looked leaner and sleeker, and Chester superhumanly strong. His wide back flexed powerfully. His arms looked as thick as nautical rope. He moved as if the world ought to make way for him. Usually that bravado made him appealing, but right now it terrified me.

The boys began wrestling perilously close to the wild flames. Rish's shoe literally touched the fire. Seeing that, Pablo stood up and tried to plant himself between them. Mel got up, too.

"Stop!" she yelled. "The last thing we need is another person getting hurt."

To my surprise, the boys heeded her command. Chester, chastened, put down a conch shell he'd wanted to throw into the fire. Rish sat beside his sister. She leaned into him affectionately. I enjoyed watching the twins together. They were about the same height and seemed to mirror each other's beauty. They also communicated effortlessly—without even talking sometimes. I'd see them exchange meaningful looks or gestures, and wondered what they meant.

Moments later, Chester sat down on the other side of Rittika. He picked leaves and put them between her toes. She slapped his hands away playfully. I sighed. Just as the sun always sets, Rittika was always flanked by boys. On one side, Rish. On the other, one of any in a long line of admirers.

Although we had pretty well exhausted ourselves by then, Mel reminded Anne Marie, Betty, and me of our duties for the night. Hearing our plan, the boys volunteered to help. They agreed to take the next shift and patrol. Anne Marie volunteered to keep the fire going for a while. The rest of us lay down on the ground and tried to sleep. We nestled close to one another, though the air was still horribly humid, even by the fire. I struggled on the ground, twisting and turning, scraping my skin and brushing off insects. I doubted I'd be able to sleep under these circumstances. I felt totally exposed and totally vulnerable. As I gazed into the darkness of the jungle, scenes from various horror movies flashed through my head.

To get them out of my mind, I tried to think of soothing things: chicken noodle soup, the sound of rain on the rooftop of our house, the threadbare Chewbacca stuffed animal I'd had since I was a little kid. But these thoughts didn't ease my worry. My eyes kept flicking from the fire back to the murky jungle. It was all too easy to imagine beastly eyes peeping out from it.

I nearly jumped out of my skin when I heard footsteps nearby. The crackle of breaking twigs. A low voice. But then I realized it was only the boys out patrolling.

Thoughts of Chester at least distracted me from my paranoia. I remembered the very first time I'd seen him fencing, at an open house hosted by the Drake Rosemont boys' and girls' fencing teams. Knowing he'd be there, I'd dragged Mel to the third floor of the gym and signed our names on an attendance sheet.

That night I was under no illusion that I'd be able to get Chester's attention. He was gorgeous, after all, and I was what I was: skinny, prone to acne, not particularly athletic, and tongue-tied at the sight of him. But my logic was this: If I joined the fencing team, I could at least watch him on a daily basis.

For weeks, Mel and I had worked on fencing basics: footwork, bladework, lunges, target practice on a wall-mounted bull's-eye. To get in better shape, we had to run up and down flights of stairs, play leapfrog, skip rope, and do so many sit-ups, pull-ups, and push-ups our bodies ached. When Coach Coifman had finally deemed us fit, we got to fence. To my surprise, I learned that I loved the absolute concentration fencing required. When I planned and executed an attack, all the other junk that normally cluttered my brain fell by the wayside.

I fenced against anyone who would have me: boys, girls, freshmen, seniors, veterans, and amateurs. One day I found myself on the fencing strip with Rittika, captain of the girls' team. At first, she took it easy on me. She even gave me some pointers. I racked up several points easily, too easily, and still she made no move to strike. Just as I gained confidence, though, she changed. Her blade was suddenly forceful, her attack precise and ruthless.

By then I'd received hundreds of touches and lashes, but this one felt different. Rittika went hard at my shoulder. I lost my balance, landing on my backside. I cried out more in embarrassment than pain. Chester, captain of the boys' team, rushed to my side. I didn't want my first contact with him to involve whimpering and shame, but I didn't have any choice. He pulled me up to my feet. I removed my mask, wiped the tears from my eyes, and tried to retain some semblance of dignity.

"Come on," he said. "There's ice packs in the equipment room."

As I followed him, I swear I saw Rittika smirk.

The third-floor equipment room was large and maze-like, not so much one room as a long, wide corridor with alleys of storage space on either side. The fencing area was at the very end of the corridor. A hodgepodge of masks, sneakers, gloves, cables, blades, and scoring machines teetered on towering industrial shelves. Fluorescent bulbs, evenly spaced along the ceiling, offered cold, stark light. The room stank of sweat and dirty laundry. I couldn't think of a less romantic place to be, and yet I felt a high-voltage charge of excitement. Despite my shoulder, despite my tear-streaked face, I was thrilled to have a moment alone with Chester.

He rifled through a cooler and found a blue plastic freeze pack. He pressed it to my shoulder, then told me to hold it there.

"You have a plastron?" he asked.

"Plastron?" I said weakly.

"You should have a plastron." He looked at me steadily. His eyes were kind, yet serious. In my daydreams I'd pictured them as blue. They were gray. "I'm surprised Rittika didn't give you one."

With a sigh, he retrieved a box from a shelf. It occurred to me that he had escorted me here not because of any latent desire to be alone with me, but because he was trying to be responsible. I was an obligation, that was all. The realization stung as much as the ache in my shoulder.

"*This* is a plastron," he announced, holding what looked like a cropped white shirt cut in half.

"Oh."

"You're supposed to wear this every time you practice."

I nodded mutely.

"Go on, then. Put it on."

I started to put it over my uniform. "No, no," he said. "It goes under your jacket."

More embarrassed than ever, I took off my fencing jacket. Underneath, my sports bra was soaked with sweat. Even worse—it had nothing to support. It would have been impossible for me to feel any more self-conscious than I did right then. I struggled to put on the plastron, unsure of where a dangling, Velcro-tipped strip was supposed to go. Chester reached behind my back, his arms around me for a moment, then secured the strip across my chest.

"There you go," he said, still close. I dared to look up at his expression. It was completely neutral.

"Thanks," I whispered. He took a small step back and looked at my face.

"You related to Rish and Rittika?"

Now it was my turn to sigh. "That's right—all of us Indians are cousins."

"All right, silly question! Not all billion of you can be related. You just look a little like Rittika is all."

I hesitated. On the one hand, I was offended by his assumption. It was a sore point for me. I was frequently held up against the handful of Indians enrolled at Drake Rosemont, as if we were all interchangeable. On the other hand, I couldn't help but take the comparison to Rittika, the prettiest girl at school, as a compliment.

"I think it's more that *she* looks a little like *me*," I said, surprised at myself.

He laughed. "Well, listen, Samantha. You remember to wear your plastron, okay? It'll save you from bruises like the one you're gonna have for the next couple of weeks. Another piece of advice: Don't underestimate Rittika. She's the girls' captain for a reason: She's a beast!"

Was she ever, I thought.

He held my gaze, and again I was struck by the sincerity of his expression. It was entirely possible, I thought, that Chester Motega was a nice person. A regular person. What a revelation.

I wanted to ask him more questions, like what kind of music did he listen to, did he have brothers or sisters, what was his favorite flavor of ice cream, did he want to meet me in the soccer field that night where we could gaze at the stars and make out? But in a flash, he turned and started walking toward the exit. I followed, pressing a freeze pack to my shoulder and staring at his butt.

I smiled at the recollection, lost briefly in memory, but then remembered what was happening. Whatever issues I had at Drake Rosemont were nothing compared to what I was facing now. I stared at the fire, wondering and worrying when my shift would start. Maybe I should get up and find out, but I was too nervous to move.

The next thing I knew, minutes had passed—or hours? I must have fallen asleep. What awakened me was not the boys telling me it was time to start my shift, or a rescuer coming to save us.

It was a chilling cry for help.

FIVE

I SAT BOLT UPRIGHT. WHAT AWFUL THING HAD happened now—had another classmate died?

My first thought was that it was Anne Marie. But I soon learned it was Avery who was in trouble. Everyone crowded around her; even the boys returned. We tried to make sense of what she was saying through chokes and sobs. Something about being touched. Touched *down there*. In the light of the campfire, her face was a teary mask of terror. She wrapped her arms around herself and shivered.

"Calm down, it's all right now," Betty said soothingly. "Tell us what happened."

"I heard this sound, this chittering sound," Avery sputtered. "And then . . . and then . . ."

"And then what?"

"He crawled over my legs. A man. A man got on top of me and tried to . . . to touch me."

The final words came out in a spasm.

"I'm so sorry—I took a break. I guess I fell asleep," whispered Anne Marie, tears streaming down her face.

Mel ignored her. "Are you sure it was a man?" she asked

Avery. Unlike everyone else, Mel stood at a distance. "Could it have been a monkey? There are a bunch of them around . . ."

"It *wasn't* a monkey," Avery spat. "It was bigger than that."

"You saw him?"

"I didn't see him. I—I felt him."

"Maybe it was a gorilla," Betty suggested. "They're big."

Through the firelight we looked to Mel, who shook her head. "It wasn't a gorilla. Gorillas live in Africa. I don't know where we are, but I know it's not Africa."

"None of you are listening! I said it was a man!"

"I believe you," Pablo told her gently.

"Listen, Avery," Betty said. "You shouldn't be scared. There are a lot of us. Nothing else is gonna happen"

"Yeah," agreed Pablo. "We'll take care of each other."

Avery nodded dolefully, then crawled beside Rittika and laid her head on her lap. Rittika stroked her hair like she was petting a dog. Most of the others gathered around them, talking quietly.

Meanwhile, Mel pulled me aside. She and I whispered about who the man could have been—a native of wherever we were? Warren, stumbling blindly through the darkness?

"But if it was Warren," Mel whispered, "why didn't he stop?"

I didn't sleep after that. I don't think anyone else did either. We took turns feeding the fire, guarding the area, and comforting Avery. Teary and inconsolable, Anne Marie wandered off. Just as we resolved to go looking for her, she came back. I could tell something else was wrong—she was unfocused, her mind seemed far away. But she wouldn't open up. The most she said was that she needed to be alone.

Mel, Pablo, Chester, and Rish took the fencing swords and circled Conch Lake, looking for signs of an intruder. They found nothing. By daybreak we were all nerves, keyed up and glassy-eyed. We should have been exhausted. Instead, we were high on adrenaline and fear.

I walked along the edge of the jungle as the sun began to rise. My bones felt brittle, as though I might break if pushed too hard. I started to think about my sister. I wondered if this was the way she felt at home: lost, scared, susceptible to things she couldn't control.

The early morning light brought a riot of birds. Their fierce squawking sounded like shattering glass. They flapped and whirled overhead, a living rainbow of magenta, neon green, tangerine, and violet—nothing like the drab-colored sparrows, mourning doves, and wrens I was used to. Somehow, their alien beauty put me even more on edge.

I went over to Mel, who was by the side of the lake sucking on a mango skin. Some of the birds began diving into the water, grabbing fish with their beaks.

"Did you get any sleep?" I asked her.

She snorted. "What about you?"

"Not really. Hey, do you still think it was a monkey?"

Her lips, wet with mango juice, puckered. "I'm not sure, Rockwell."

"So it's possible it was a man?"

"I looked at the footprints on that little beach over there," she said, pointing to the same place I'd sat yesterday. "Ours were there, but there was another set, too."

"Another set?"

"They were so weird—kind of human, but the toes had—I don't know—claws. Or talons. Tracking with my dad, I've never seen prints like that."

"Maybe it was a yeti," I said, hoping a joke would offset my fear.

"Maybe."

"We could finally catch Big Foot."

She snorted again, then said, "Honestly, it's not just the prints I'm worried about. Something went missing last night. Chester's shoes. He took them off after he lay down. But in the morning, they were gone."

I felt the nausea of yesterday return with a vengeance. "You don't think it was the monkeys?"

"Rockwell, we can't blame the monkeys for everything."

A bird plunged like a bullet into the water, impaling a fish with its beak. As it ascended, the fish was still flopping. I made out a blot of crimson on its gleaming, silvery scales. Mel tossed the mango peel into Conch Lake. It floated like a misshapen ship, drifting in slow circles.

"Rittika thinks we'll be rescued this morning," I said.

Mel shrugged noncommittally.

"Do you think we will?"

"Like my dad says, 'Hope for the best, prepare for the worst.'"

I, too, remembered Mr. Sharpe's words. But I never thought they would apply to someone like me, in a situation like this.

"Get something to eat," she told me, squeezing my wrist. "Who knows what this day's gonna be like?"

When she left to attend to the fire, I scouted for a couple of bananas. Then I joined Pablo and Anne Marie. They were sitting on some big pink boulders, eating their own fruit. I was struck by how quiet they were, as if they were waiting. For rescuers? For someone to tell them what to do?

Anne Marie gave me a bashful smile when she saw me. When I returned her smile, though, she abruptly turned away and stared into the jungle. By the look on her face, I'd say she was mesmerized by it. Wordlessly, Pablo broke off pieces of a peeled mango and handed them to me. I offered him half a banana in return. Together, we gazed at Conch Lake.

"It's kind of beautiful here," he said, "if you don't count the mosquitoes . . ."

"Or the madman on the loose," I added.

He chuckled. "I can't believe how untouched it is. I didn't even know places like this existed."

"Me neither."

"It's kind of reassuring, given how messed up the rest of the world is."

I understood where he was coming from. Pablo was the guy on the fencing team who was always reminding us to recycle our soda cans and to stop buying plastic water bottles. Sometimes he handed us petitions to sign. *Stop offshore drilling. Urge your legislators to outlaw pesticides. Save dolphins from being tangled to death in fishing nets.* He was pretty intense when it came to environmental stuff. So it was surprising that he and Chester were good friends and roommates. Chester was all about having fun and goofing off, while Pablo was serious, someone who thought deeply about the world. Most of the time when I saw Pablo, he was reading, lost in information and the music coming out of his earbuds.

"I heard there isn't a single place left in the world that hasn't been touched by pollution," he said. "But maybe Conch Lake is the exception."

"Maybe," I replied, eating another piece of mango.

We continued to chew and stare at our surroundings. I noticed the clouds above Conch Lake start to turn gray and fat. Minutes later, lightning crackled and the jungle grew curiously quiet. A raindrop fell on my knee, followed by ten more. The downpour that followed extinguished the fire in an instant. It drenched our hair, our clothes, our food, our voices. The storm had come on even faster than the one yesterday.

Mel scurried to tuck her backpack inside a horizontal crevice between the rocks. Anne Marie squeezed shut her eyes, as if she could will the storm away. Rittika and some of the other girls held their school jackets over their heads, but it didn't matter. Wind lashed the rain in all directions. There was no way to stay dry. To be heard over the pelting wet, we had to scream.

"Number one priority is exploration—finding Warren, finding equipment, and finding out where the hell we are," Mel yelled. "Number two is shelter. Dry shelter."

"I think we should stay where we are," Rittika screamed back. "All of us. When help comes, they'll find Warren."

"But when will help come? Yesterday, you were scared Rish might be injured. What if Warren is?"

They went back and forth like this for what felt like forever, until Rish intervened, siding with his sister, motioning to the sky, as if the rain were a sign from heaven that we ought to stay put. Mel wouldn't have it. She said she was going, even if no one else would.

"I agree with Mel," Chester shouted, water ricocheting off his face. He wasn't wearing his shirt, and drops flew off the hard planes of his body, too.

Pablo added, "I'm also with Mel. Warren could be hurt. What kind of friends are we if we don't look for him?"

Rish and Rittika whispered to each other intensely. Finally, they agreed to go with Mel's plan. But judging from Rittika's sour face, she wasn't happy about it.

Mel assigned search teams: Rish and Rittika would travel east, Mel and I west, and Chester and Pablo north, up a mountain in the distance. When Rittika complained that she didn't know which way was east, Mel explained how we could inspect tree bark and look at the location of anthills. Rittika's response was to roll her eyes. She didn't understand—and neither did anybody else.

Fortunately, the rain began to ease up. When the sun was out again, Mel showed us how to tell direction with a "shadow stick." My teammates observed her closely as she made a kind of natural compass with a long, straight stick stuck in the ground. I figured I didn't have to pay much attention since Mel was my partner.

To tell you the truth, it was always this way—Mel talking, me taking a backseat.

Once the teams knew where to go, Mel advised Avery, Betty, Ming, and Anne Marie to stay behind and get the fire going again. She handed one of Chester's swords to each of them.

"Gather more food and whatever else might be of use nearby. Do your best to build a basic shelter."

Avery and Ming nodded skeptically. I could tell they didn't feel up to the challenge.

"Are we clear?" Mel asked.

"We'll do our best," Betty replied, raising her chin.

"Good. We'll meet you back here before sundown," Mel said.

"Back here at Camp Summerbliss," Rittika said with a sniff.

Camp Summerbliss.

I couldn't help but smile. Obviously, Rittika was being ironic—*bliss* was hardly a word that jumped to mind under our circumstances. Even so, the name stuck in my head, the same way Conch Lake had.

One by one, we took long drinks from the outcrop, then set off. I followed Mel as she charged into the jungle. She kept a brisk pace but, after a few minutes, stopped in front of a tree. It had a distinctive double trunk, forking into a V. Mel gestured to a mark carved neatly in the bark.

"Who made that? You?" I asked.

"Yeah."

"Why?"

"To keep a tally of the days we're here."

"Is that really necessary? I mean, we're going to be rescued . . ."

"I'm keeping it just in case."

"In case of what?"

"In case no rescuers show up. Days can start to blend together when there's no record of them."

That wasn't the answer I wanted to hear.

Mel took the fake eye from her sock and dropped it carefully between the tree's forked limbs. It sat there comfortably in a little indentation in the bark. I don't know why Mel decided to put it there. I wished she hadn't. Out in the open, that eye gave me the creeps. I'd never admit it to Mel, but I wondered if it could see us somehow, if it was full of magic, or worse, bad luck.

We kept going, calling out for Warren. Our westward journey seemed to be taking us up. I sensed the perpetual, gradual elevation in my hamstrings and calf muscles. After a couple of hours, we began to leave the jungle behind. The trees and canopy thinned, and the air tasted different—less chokingly muggy. Here and there, pink crags poked out of the earth like stalagmites. Like the rocks around Conch Lake, they were a mishmash of minerals.

"Mica, quartz, and feldspar," Mel said knowledgeably. I remembered the rock and mineral collection in her father's study.

Threaded around the crags were thickly knitted creepers. Mel and I moved carefully. We had to stop frequently to untangle our feet. After a few stumbles, I tripped, scraping my knee. On the ground, I was face-to-face with the impossibly dense undergrowth, a labyrinth of roots and stems.

Mel crouched beside me. She touched a bead of blood on my skin with her finger and wiped it on her blouse.

"I wish we had hiking boots."

"I'd rather have a machete," I said.

"Maybe time for a break?"

"Definitely."

We ate some fruit she'd put in her backpack. We weren't really hungry, though, just thirsty. The rain already felt like a distant memory. The sun sizzled through the last wispy clouds. Today would be another scorcher.

When we continued, we kept our eyes focused on the ground to avoid further stumbles. Here and there, we noticed narrow paths in the undergrowth. These were neat and tidy, as if made by a miniature plow. They were just large enough for Mel and me to eel through, but most didn't extend very far. They seemed to start and end at random points, without planning or purpose. I couldn't make sense of them.

I walked more confidently in the paths, without fear of stumbling, but Mel looked uncertain. When she stopped in front of a small brown mound, her uncertainty turned to worry.

"What is it?" I asked her.

"Scat."

"What?"

"*Scat*. It's another word for poop." She gestured toward the mound.

"I blame the monkeys."

"You always blame the monkeys."

" 'Cause I don't want to think of the alternative."

"Whatever made this was bigger than a monkey, Rockwell. Way bigger." She kicked at the scat with the toe of her shoe. "It's fresh," she added.

I didn't know what to do with this information. All I knew was that it was bad, and that Mel was concerned. She was no longer marching, but treading slowly. Watchfully. The mystery animal was still on our minds when we came to a bluff. Before us was a spectacular view of water glistening in the sunlight.

Ocean. It surrounded us on all sides. We were on an island.

"Crappity crap crap," Mel gasped.

My jaw dropped as I stared. Along the shoreline, the water was crystal clear. I could make out pearly, rippled dunes on the ocean floor. Farther out, a shadow, probably a reef, encircled much of the island, and at the outer edges of that shadow, long fingers of sea foam tapered into deeper water. The South Pacific. It was endless, inching to the horizon.

The view was one of the most beautiful I'd ever seen. And one of the most terrifying.

"We'd better be rescued, Rockwell," Mel whispered. "Otherwise, I don't know how we'll get out of this one."

"We won't be able to walk home, that's for sure," I replied.

"We won't be able to swim there either. There's no other land in sight."

We stared at the vast ocean for a long time before turning our attention to the island. It was both scary and fascinating to take stock of it from this vantage point. We were at a high elevation, though not as high as what lay to the north: the mountain Chester and Pablo must by now be climbing. From where we stood, we could make out the island's major features: pink granite along the mountainside, an emerald forest that dominated its interior, Conch Lake studding its center like a peacock-colored jewel. Mel said the shape of the island reminded her of a fish's shape: blunt on the "head" end with the curve of the beach, thin on the "tail" end with two forked points. Just beyond those points, a separate outcrop poked up out of the water.

I began to feel dizzy. Maybe the lack of sleep was catching up with me. Or maybe I had gone physically and mentally beyond my limits. I touched the top of my head, surprised at how hot my hair felt. Then again, the sun had been beating on it all morning. My face, too, felt alarmingly warm. As for Mel, she was a walking reminder to wear sunscreen. Her face was the color of a tomato.

We decided to return to Camp Summerbliss. It was hard to say what time it was, but we'd been walking for a long time. It was definitely past noon. Mel suggested taking a different route home. It might be faster. And even if it wasn't, the scat had spooked her.

I'd hoped the journey back, on a decline, would be easier. It wasn't. Although my leg muscles no longer throbbed, loose rocks rolled out from underneath my feet, creating miniature avalanches. I had to watch every step. Carefully, Mel and I wended our way through more creepers. To our dismay, we soon encountered more paths. I walked ahead of my friend down a particularly long one. I was staring at the ground, so I didn't see at first that we had company.

A pig.

Ungainly and wild, it looked both frightened and frightening. It was a bulky, bristly, mangy thing, with curved tusks at the corners of its mouth. Its head was narrow, its pebbly eyes too close together. I froze. The pig let out an unhappy squeal and scratched its hooves fretfully against the ground. As it came closer, I could smell it. Manure mingled with wet dog.

I turned my head toward Mel, looking for help. That's when it charged at me, hard, hurling its weight into my right leg. For an instant, I felt the squishy, spongy wet of its snout against my bare skin. Then my knee buckled, and the pain seared. I careened to the ground, falling into the spiky creepers. I didn't know if I'd broken a bone, twisted an ankle. I wished I'd had time to think, but the pig was ready for more. It scuttled back onto the path and scratched at the dirt, aggressively now, sending little puffs of dust into the air. Its eyes were trained on me. Between shock, the pain in my knee, and the way the creepers entangled me, I struggled to move. The best I could do was shield my face.

Through a chink in my fingers, I watched Mel react. She fished around in her sock, producing a switchblade. She clicked it open and whipped it through the air. The steel blade caught the sunlight, and flashed. Then she tore after the creature, squealing and hoofing as it had. It looked up at her in dismay, and I partially pitied it, pitied the terror on its homely face. She swiped the blade across its side as it attempted to turn around, its legs scrabbling, its pudgy body squirming and twitching, trying in vain to push through the dense tangle. Mel had a chance to knife it again—I could see her debating whether she should, but she wiped the bloody blade against her sock instead. The injured creature finally made headway into the creepers. Another squeal, and then its backside and tufted tail disappeared into the undergrowth.

Shuddering, I moved my hands from my face. I stared at Mel. I tried to breathe. The pig's blood looked bright and alarming against the grimy cotton of her sock.

"Will it die?" I whispered.

"I didn't get it very deep. I should have killed it. Killed it before it killed you."

I swallowed the lump in my throat.

"It was a boar," Mel said. "My father sees them in Borneo. He says the ones there have beards. Funny, huh?" I couldn't believe how offhanded, how cavalier she sounded, but that was Mel for you.

She helped me to break free from the creepers. I swore they'd already started to twine around me, as if I was just another bothersome obstacle in their way.

"A knife, Mel? You're full of surprises."

She shrugged.

"That's how you carved the notch in the tree, right? Do you always carry it with you?"

"You never know what the day will bring."

I raised my eyebrows, but I wasn't truly surprised. Of course Mel would carry a switchblade. I wouldn't be shocked if the other Sharpe sisters carried bayonets and nunchucks. That was just the way things were in the Sharpe house. Mel clicked the knife back into its bed and tucked it in her sock. It disappeared against the thick bulge of her calf.

When I'd caught my breath, we moved on. Mel walked ahead this time; I limped behind, more scared than ever. We encountered a relatively easy stretch and then, at Mel's insistence, veered toward a beach. It was as lovely up close as it had been from a distance. The white sand was fine and soft as sugar, flecked with bits of broken shell and coral. There was a surprising amount of washed-up garbage, too. But I didn't mind it so much when I saw the water.

The waves were inviting as they lapped gently ashore. When they pulled away, they left frothy trails, paler even than the sand. I ran in up to my knees, then dove beneath the surface, keeping under for as long as I could, letting the salt clean my wounds. When I came up, I saw Mel watching from the shore. She was sitting on the sand, shielding her face with a palm frond.

I waved for her to come in, but she shook her head. I stayed, swimming, floating, diving, trying—literally—to wash away some of my anxiety. When I finally hauled myself out, Mel had relocated upshore, to a shady patch beneath a trio of palm trees.

"I'm starving," I told her. She unearthed a granola bar from the depths of her backpack. Snapping it in two, she gave me half.

"I've been saving it for a special moment," she said.

It was the best damn granola bar I'd ever had.

After I'd eaten, I made a move to get up, but stopped dead when Mel gasped. I had a terrible feeling that another boar was approaching. Slowly, I turned in the direction Mel was staring. Nearby, in the shadow of another clutch of palm trees, was indeed an animal. But it wasn't a boar.

It was a bird. A huge bird, almost the size of an ostrich. Its proportions were cartoonish: long, sturdy legs and little wings, fat body, and jaunty tail. I doubted its tiny wings could propel it off the ground. They were more like ornamental flippers.

Vestigial. The word popped into my head. Mr. Sharpe would have been proud—he was surely the person I'd heard it from.

"That bird is supposed to be extinct," Mel whispered under her breath.

"What?"

"Extinct," she repeated. "It's an ibis. A Réunion ibis."

"Oh, yes!" I said, too loudly, for I remembered suddenly

what a Réunion ibis was. During one of my summers at Mel's house, Mr. Sharpe had built a diorama of Réunion island. It was one of a group of islands located in the Indian Ocean, close to the African coast. He had plenty to say about Réunion, which was a favorite from his travels. A beautiful, warm place, perhaps not unlike where we found ourselves now.

Mel, her sisters, and I had helped Mr. Sharpe put the diorama together, molding mountains out of chicken wire and papier-mâché, painting forests, making animals out of clay. Mr. Sharpe told us that hundreds of species inhabited the island, and many lived nowhere else in the world. Unfortunately, some had also gone extinct, including the Réunion ibis. I remember being saddened when Mr. Sharpe showed us a painting of one in a book and told us its story. Waddling and mild, like a dodo, the ibis had been hunted to extinction by the eighteenth century. It had been too gullible, too easy to lure and kill.

"A shame," he'd said. "Gone before its time, like the mammoth and mastodon."

And yet, this creature taken for dead was here now, unmistakably. It looked exactly like the image in the book.

Mel opened her backpack and found the other half of the granola bar. A precious resource, but Mel couldn't resist. She broke off a piece and walked very slowly and quietly toward the bird. It took a step back, but halted when it saw what was in Mel's hand. Without hesitation, it shambled up to her.

"Here you go, pretty one. That's it. Come and get it," she murmured.

The ibis ate straight from her palm. Its beak was sharp; it could have bitten off a finger if it wanted to. But it took the food gently. I wasn't surprised to see a tear running down my friend's cheek. I knew why. Mel wished her father could see this.

As quietly as I could, I approached the ibis, too. It eyed me, but made no motion to move.

"This is unbelievable, Rockwell."

"You're telling me."

After Mel gave the ibis the rest of the bar, it peered at us expectantly. It reminded me of a dog waiting for a treat. Mel and I began to laugh. I honestly couldn't remember a more magical moment. The ibis, the ocean, the lull of the waves, even the graceful shapes of the palm tree shadows on the sand: Nothing could have been improved upon. The only other time I had experienced this kind of magic was at Mel's house in Maine during summers and school vacations.

Though I worried about Alexa, those periods at the Sharpe house were the happiest of my life. Being part of the Sharpe household was bliss. There is no other word for it. When Mel's father was home, back from another exotic place, he'd always summon Mel, her sisters, and me to his workshop.

"Look at the wings of this butterfly," he'd say, adjusting the lens of his heavy black microscope. "I've never seen iridescence like this."

The girls would get in line, me in the middle of the mix. With Mr. Sharpe as our tutor, we saw so many treasures from nature: honeycomb, coral, snakeskins, vials of pollen, garnets, insects and small animals pickled in spirits. As we took turns admiring the latest find, Mr. Sharpe would share fascinating tidbits he'd learned. Everything from how to extract poison from a blowfish to what to do if a polar bear attacks. I'd never heard him unable to answer a question, or unwilling to look for the answer.

In his workshop, an enormous, gabled room overflowing with curiosities, Mr. Sharpe placed in our hands pelts, bones, fossils, crumbling pieces of pottery, tribal masks, Egyptian scarabs, arrowheads, shells from every ocean and sea. We handled these marvels gingerly, our faces calm even if our hearts were pounding right out of our chests. The workshop was a zoo, museum, curio case, and heaven all at once. In it, I'd petted the hairy legs of a live tarantula, held the bony jaw of a great white shark, and pinned dead moths to a display board. Mel, her sisters, and I were welcome to be whatever we wanted to be: naturalists, geographers, archaeologists, world-class explorers. We'd close our eyes, twirl the globe in the middle of the workshop, and point. Wherever our fingers ended up was where we pretended to go, together. One big all-girl expedition team.

At night in our pajamas, we lay on the flat rooftop above the porch, or we camped outdoors in tents, trapping fireflies in jars and searching for night crawlers. Sometimes we toured Mrs. Sharpe's greenhouse by flashlight, gazing at her newest sprouts and seedlings. Deep into the evening, Mr. Sharpe told us stories by a campfire. He'd had a million adventures—running for his life from flesh-eating ants in the Amazon, dodging a trampling herd of elephants in India, watching Maori faces being tattooed in New Zealand.

He was a wonderful, animated storyteller. I never tired of listening to him, or watching him gesture and mime his way through a tale. Nor did I find his style of dress "better suited to a younger man," as my mother had once said. Every day he dressed as if for a journey, with scuffed boots and a satchel tossed over a shoulder. His clothes had pockets for all his supplies: knife, notebook and pencil, compass, magnifying glass, spyglass, one flask for water and another for brandy ("a natural antiseptic," Mr. Sharpe said). He took these supplies everywhere he went, even if it was just the pharmacy or grocery store.

He called me "girl" most of the time, as in "Come here, girl, look at this!" or "Did you hear that birdcall, girl?" I was never sure, even after a dozen visits, if Mr. Sharpe knew my name. To be fair, he confused his daughters' names, too. But his absent-mindedness didn't bother me because he made up for it. Mr. Sharpe was the most attentive adult I'd ever met, hands down. He thought nothing of taking off a whole morning to show Mel how to tie knots, or to take Tasman to collect salamander eggs.

Given that he had a house full of girls, I'd once asked Mr. Sharpe if he wished he'd had a son.

He'd chuckled, admitting, "Can't say I ever thought about it."

That made me love him even more.

Oh, how I envied those Sharpe girls! What did it feel like to have a father like that? My father spent as little time with Alexa and me as he could. And when he did make time, it was usually to lecture us on something. Or to make Alexa miserable.

Here's something else I envied about those five ruddy-cheeked Sharpe girls: They didn't care how they looked. Between them, they didn't own a single lipstick or hand mirror. One brush and comb satisfied the lot of them. After being around Mel and her sisters, it was difficult for me to go back to my mother, who fixated on her looks through a medicated haze, ignoring the important stuff. Like how Alexa wore only long sleeves. Or how she drank tamarind sauce to disguise the vomit smell of her breath, and sprayed half a bottle of air freshener in the bathroom every time she went in.

I cried for my sister sometimes when I came back from Maine. I cried because I knew there was a different way to live, and she didn't. I alone had been part of the Sharpe tribe, whooping and hollering and running amok, five blondes and one brunette, all of us clutching birch spears we'd whittled ourselves. All of us ecstatically free.

SIX

I'D HOPED AGAINST HOPE THAT WARREN WOULD BE waiting for us at Camp Summerbliss when we got back. But there was no sign of him, or rescuers, either. Yet there were changes. Betty, Avery, Ming, and Anne Marie had improved our temporary living situation. Now there was a tidy ring of rocks around the campfire and a spit on thick stick sawhorses for roasting the conch meat. Most impressive of all, the girls had woven a large tarp out of grass and plant fibers. It was draped over the horizontal branch of a nearby tree. Anchored with stones, it formed a tent as green as the jungle.

"It's a basic shelter, like Mel wanted. The weave's tight, but I can't guarantee it's waterproof," Betty said, walking me around it. "At least it'll be shady during the day, though."

"This is incredible," I told her.

"My aunt's a weaver. She has a loom in her house. I guess I've learned a thing or two."

And there was more. Betty led me to where the boulders began their ascent to the outcrop. Betty and her team had created a makeshift kitchen on the flatter rocks. One "table" held smashed conch shells, another held a heaping pile of clean meat, and a third was designated for eating, with woven mats for plates and sticks roughly hewn into two-pronged forks.

"Betty, I had no idea you were so handy!"

She chewed on her lip as she explained, "I did it to stay busy. If I let myself think about what's going on, I'll fall apart."

She looked at her injured arm for a moment, then continued, her voice dropping. "Speaking of falling apart, I'm worried about Anne Marie. She's been crying all day . . . and mumbling."

"Mumbling about what?"

"I don't know. I couldn't make it out. I tried to calm her down, but she . . ."

Before she could say more, Rish, Rittika, Pablo, and Chester came charging out of the jungle with flushed faces and fearful eyes.

"It's bad," Rittika said, looking at us. "Real bad."

"What is?"

"All day, Ritt and I have been calling out Warren's name," Rish said. "Man, we've been everywhere. Ritt didn't think we'd find him, but we did."

The way he said it sent shivers up and down my spine.

"Show us where," Mel said.

"No way! I'm not going back there," Rittika replied, slipping her arm through her brother's.

"He's dead, isn't he?" Mel asked.

I looked at the twins, and saw that she'd guessed right. Rish wiped his eyes, which were rapidly filling with tears.

"You have to show us," Mel insisted.

Others started crying, too—Betty and Pablo.

"How far away is he?" Mel asked.

"I don't know—an hour's walk, maybe less," Rish replied.

Nervously, Mel glanced at the patch of sky over Conch Lake. "Let's go. We can make it back by sundown if we hurry."

There was no more discussion, just a flurry of bodies heading back into the abyss of the jungle. Surprisingly, Rittika didn't follow her brother as he and Mel took off. But I did. I'm not sure what drove me. I'd like to think it was concern—concern for a schoolmate—but in truth, it was probably the need to be near Mel. Chester, Pablo, and Betty followed, too. In hushed, cautious voices, we shared what we'd learned that day. Mel and I talked about the wild boar, the ibis, and the realization that we were island-bound. Chester and Pablo had also seen the surrounding water, but they'd been equally focused on another discovery.

"At the top of the mountain, there were caves," Chester said. "Made of the same pink rock that's everywhere around here. Most of the openings were too small to get through. But a few were bigger. We got down on our hands and knees and crawled through one. About twenty feet in, we came to an open space. We could stand up, no problem. But it was very dark. We couldn't see, so we turned back."

"Were there any signs of other people?" Mel asked. "Clothing, tools, anything like that?"

"Like Chester said, we couldn't see anything," Pablo replied. "But I guess there could have been something . . . or someone."

Chester positioned himself beside Mel, matching her furious pace. "We have to tell you something else," he said. "We saw something up in a tree, like an old parachute or something, tangled in the branches. There was a bundle hanging off it. We could make it out through the leaves."

"It was really high up," Pablo added. "I don't know how we'd get it down."

There was a sudden light, a spark of hope, in Mel's otherwise grim expression. "Maybe it has supplies in it," she murmured.

"We might be able to climb that tree," Chester said. "*Might*. But I won't lie—it would be tough."

"If things don't turn around soon, we're not going to have any choice but to try."

Rish told us that he and Rittika had stumbled upon shoreline early on. They'd thought about going swimming off some rocks, but had seen a fin cutting through the water.

"A shark, a big one," Rish said. "On the way back, we picked through some plane wreckage. Everything was charred. Forget your dream of a radio, Mel. But we did come across something—a bad smell, like rotten eggs. We followed it till it got stronger, and finally we figured out it was coming from a black pond. I've never seen—or smelled—anything like it."

Mel looked at him thoughtfully. I could almost see the wheels in her head turning.

"I bet the smell was methane gas," she said.

Despite our somberness, Chester chuckled. "Methane? As in . . ."

"Yeah, as in farts," she conceded. "It sounds like Rish found himself a tar pit."

"Damn," Rish said. "This island's got a little of everything."

"Yeah, except rescuers," I complained.

"They'll come," Betty said, patting me on the shoulder.

"My father once took me and my sisters to see tar pits—La Brea," Mel said. "They're in California. The tar's been around forever, and it's trapped all kinds of creatures, even dinosaurs. Animals come to drink the water on the top, then fall in."

"They just sink?" asked Rish.

"Yep. And the bones are kept intact because tar happens to be an excellent preservative."

She paused, those wheels still turning. "Later, I'd like to see this tar pit of yours."

Chester scratched at a mosquito bite and said, "Up on the mountaintop, the island felt small. But down here, back in the jungle, it feels big again."

"It's a decent-size place," Mel replied. "I don't know why we haven't seen signs of other people."

I noticed she didn't mention the strange, taloned footprint.

I became aware of the fact that Pablo and I were walking side by side, in lockstep. I was grateful for his closeness, for the faint suggestion of security.

When our group reached the shore, Rish warned us that what we were about to see was disturbing. But I had no idea just how terrible it would be.

Warren lay on the white sand, bloated and contorted. His

face looked entirely different: broader, duller, doughy. His mouth hung open, slack-jawed, almost like he was sleeping. His eyes were open, too. Their color had faded to something bland and indistinct. His clothes were tattered and askew. I had a feeling he'd been picked at by animals—birds, maybe even boars.

It was surreal to see him like this. Our friend. A nice, mellow guy whom everyone liked. I don't know how long he'd been dead, but his body was baking under the hot sun—and decomposing. The rancid stink hit me as far as ten feet away. Closer, it was intolerable. I put my hands over my nose and mouth, and willed myself not to throw up.

"Oh my god," Rish said. "That wasn't there before."

It took me a second to realize what he meant. A couple of yards away from Warren was a note written in huge, misshapen, almost childish writing on the sand.

LEAVE OR DIE.

"Are you sure it wasn't there?" Mel said. "Maybe you didn't notice it . . . maybe you didn't see past Warren . . ."

"No. Goddamn it, it wasn't there. I swear! I would've seen it. Rittika would've seen it."

"So someone was here in between the time you and your sister were here, and now?" Pablo asked.

"If that's true, then we're being watched," said Mel.

Rish shuddered, turned slowly, and stared into the dark, leafy labyrinth of the jungle.

Mel strode over to Warren's body. She examined him with

the same directness and detachment with which she'd examined Jeremiah. I could barely watch.

She rolled him over and went through his pockets. If she had hoped to find anything, she had to be disappointed. Nothing to see here but death and the note. I have to admit that those three words scared me just as much as the sight of Warren. *LEAVE OR DIE* was more than a warning. It seemed to me like a promise.

I found myself leaning against Pablo. I wasn't sure if I could support my own weight much longer. He put his arm around my waist, literally propping me up, while Mel and Chester treaded carefully around the note. Mel studied it judiciously.

"The person who wrote this did it with his feet," she said. "See the heel prints? The indentation of the whole foot here? And look at this." Mel gestured to a series of small impressions in the sand. "I thought these were claw marks at first. But now I'm sure they're very long toenails."

She gave me a meaningful look, and I knew that these tracks were the same as the ones she'd seen by Conch Lake.

The footprints led from the jungle to the note, and back. Mel pointed out little holes, following in a straight line, next to the prints.

"I think he made them with the tip of a stick. Maybe a cane. Maybe he's injured?"

"Let's hope so," Chester said tensely.

As we considered this idea, a little monkey scampered onto the sand. Pablo swore it was the same one that had followed

Rish, Chester, and him after the crash. It scooted next to us and screeched—a sound like a seagull's scream. I wasn't sure if it was friendly or hostile.

Then, as quickly as it had appeared, it disappeared back into the jungle.

By now, night was starting to fall. Mel suggested returning to camp, but first we had to discuss *the body*. That's what Warren had already become. How quickly—how cruelly. With a shudder, I realized that I might be getting used to death. First the pilot, then Jeremiah, and now Warren. Betty was crying, but not me. There had been too many atrocities in too little time. Maybe my mind had steeled itself before it unraveled, maybe this was how soldiers became anesthetized to war.

Betty argued for a burial. She was still upset that we'd left Jeremiah in the state we'd found him. She spoke of "the right thing to do," but we voted against her, or rather, we sided with Mel, who said sharply, "Not to be cruel, but it's too late for Warren. Someone's after us. We need to think about *us*."

I agreed with her. Even so, it felt like a terrible thing to leave him there on the beach.

We didn't make it back before sundown. It was thanks to Mel's uncanny sense of direction that we made it back at all. The ones who had remained at camp were sitting around the fire, waiting anxiously for our return. They gave us fruit and smoky conch meat, but I wasn't hungry anymore. They wanted to know what had happened. They demanded answers. But we didn't have any. Only more questions.

That second night was much worse than the first. It was full of fearful shifts and antsy patrolling, of building up the fire and listening for intruders. We were sure if someone came for us, it wouldn't be a rescuer, but the writer of that message—out for blood.

It was deep in the night when I finished my rounds and finally fell into a troubled sleep. But it didn't last long. Mel nudged me awake.

"I don't think he was murdered," she whispered.

"What?"

"Warren. I think he was already dead, dead from the crash. Someone just wanted to scare us. Make us go away."

"Who—who wanted to make us go away?" I asked, not quite sure if I was dreaming.

"Whoever wrote the note," she replied. "Our enemy."

When I fell asleep again, I had nightmares—boars eating decaying flesh, a thousand black flies hovering, a cute little monkey morphing into a bloodthirsty monster.

At daybreak, I was more exhausted than ever. I noticed that my skirt was loose. In only two days, I'd lost a lot of weight. I dragged myself to the edge of Conch Lake and washed my face. Nearby, I noticed Betty rubbing her teeth clean with her finger. She'd braided her hair, too. I copied what she'd done, hoping that this bit of normalcy and routine would make me feel better. It didn't. All it felt like was a lie.

Mel came over and told me she had something to say. Then she waded into Conch Lake and called for everyone to listen.

Rittika, Avery, and Ming, who had been swimming, paddled over to her. The boys tramped out from the jungle. Betty and Anne Marie abandoned the fruit they'd been nibbling.

"Listen up!" Mel said. "I don't know how long we'll be here—hours, or days, or weeks. But if this island is our home, even for a little while, we have to take precautions. I'm talking about Conch Lake specifically. Except for rain, the waterfall is our only fresh water. It's our most valuable resource. We could find gold or diamonds, and it wouldn't matter if we didn't have clean water to drink."

"Where are you going with this?" Rittika asked, her annoyance evident.

"We need to be careful with the outcrop water, and with Conch Lake, too. It's bad enough we're all swimming there. We're contaminating it just by doing that. But if you need to go to the bathroom, stay out."

"God, Mel!" Rittika said. "What are we—toddlers? Are you going to hand out diapers next?"

"I'm just being reasonable," Mel said calmly. "It would only take one accident by one person to pollute Conch Lake—and ruin it for all of us."

Chuckling, Chester said, "I don't think you need to worry."

"Do you think so, Chester? People have said that before. 'Don't worry. It's no big deal.' But hey, waterborne diseases kill more people than war and terrorism combined. Cholera, dysentery, typhoid, hepatitis—they're all caused by polluted water."

"Yeah, but you're talking about impoverished countries, not American teenagers."

"Exactly," Mel said. "I'm talking about countries. Developing countries with their own economies, legislatures, infrastructures, and transportation systems. Countries with MBAs and scientists and doctors. They've said, 'No problem, we've got the water covered.' And you know what? Thousands of people still die from drinking and bathing in tainted water. So don't get on your high horse. A bunch of spoiled private school kids shouldn't overestimate themselves."

A hush fell over the group. I don't know how it was possible, but I suddenly felt even more anxious.

"We get it, Mel," Rittika said cynically. "Don't crap in Conch Lake."

"Good," Mel replied. "And on that note, I've designated an area of the jungle for those purposes."

Dismissively, Rittika waved off the comment.

"Can't we talk about something that actually matters?" she asked. "Like Warren—and what happened to him. That's what we should be discussing."

"I agree!" said Avery.

"Me too," added Ming.

Mel sighed.

"Yeah, there's no question that someone's after us," Chester said. "I think we should act. We need to go on the offensive. Like Coach Coifman says, the best defense is to attack."

Rittika nodded emphatically. "Yeah, absolutely."

"We have our swords. We could make spears."

Rish added excitedly, "It's only morning—we still have hours of daylight to hunt him down."

"Before we do anything," Mel interjected, "there are things to consider."

"Like what?" Rittika asked tersely.

"Like the fact that this enemy stole Chester's shoes from camp but walks around in bare feet. Why? It doesn't make any sense—unless he's not alone."

Chester shrugged. "So what if there's two of them, or three? We still have numbers on our side. Look at all of us, dude!"

Dutifully, I looked at my classmates, one by one. But seeing them didn't rouse in me a sense of confidence. In fact, quite the opposite. We were just kids. Innocent kids. We were like a school of little fish darting in dark water. A predator could easily take us out.

Though the day was warm, a light breeze off Conch Lake suddenly felt like an icy shawl about my shoulders. I shuddered, wondering how much danger still awaited us. I peered into the jungle, marveling at how many nooks and crannies it suddenly seemed to have. So many places among the shadows where someone could hunker down and sit tight, waiting to strike.

Rittika, Chester, and even Rish looked twitchy and restless, like they were ready to wage war that very second. But Mel's face was still doubtful.

"We were threatened, Mel," Chester told her. "We can't just wait here like sitting ducks."

"I didn't say we should. But we have to think through whatever plan we make."

"As long as we don't waste time," Rittika said.

"That's right." Rish nodded. "The sooner we act, the better. Before anything else happens . . ."

"Say we find this guy," Betty said. "And somehow, someway, we manage to catch him. What then?"

"We contain the threat," Chester replied.

"We make him our prisoner," Rittika added. "Torture him till he gives us answers."

"This isn't Guantanamo," Betty said.

"All's fair in love and war."

"This isn't war."

"Isn't it?" Rittika asked.

"Stop. Just stop!" Mel demanded. "We don't even know who it is, and already we're planning to torture him? That's crazy."

"I wouldn't have a problem inflicting pain if that's what it took," Chester said.

Rittika added, "He'd do it to us. He said it himself: 'Leave or die.'"

"Listen," Mel said. "I think we should start with that parachute thing Chester and Pablo found. We ought to get it down."

"That would be a waste of time!"

"No, it wouldn't. Maybe there's something there that could

help us—a weapon, a clue, anything. We need all the help we can get."

"Maybe she's right," Chester conceded.

The eyes of my friends turned toward Rittika. I knew that whatever words came out of her mouth would dictate our course. Rish, Ming, Avery—they would do whatever she said.

As for Mel's words, those were less clear. I wasn't sure if she really thought we might find something useful, or if she was simply buying time, delaying the search and keeping the angry masses at bay for a little longer, as long as she could.

Rittika toyed with a shiny lock of hair. Unlike mine, which was oily and tangled from lack of shampooing, hers still looked great. Further evidence of her physical superiority—as if I needed any more.

"All right, Mel," she said finally. "Have it your way this time. But if we don't find anything, we're going to do what *I* say."

SEVEN

WE WALKED IN A LINE THROUGH THE JUNGLE, RITTIKA
and Chester at the front. I was directly behind Mel, a position I was used to. The line itself reminded me of school. Drake Rosemont was a place that thrived on order and teemed with rules. Even its buildings stood in perfect alignment. Several times a year the grounds crew trimmed the ivy that grew on the outside walls. God forbid it grow too tangled and wild.

I thought back to three years ago—when I'd started Drake Rosemont as a high school freshman. Those first weeks had been the most confusing of my life. I'd barely understood the social code of an average public school. How was I expected to master elite Drake Rosemont, with its ceremonies and songs, its societies and slang? I felt like I needed a special dictionary just to get around. The cafeteria was a "dining hall," the grassy square at the center of campus a "quad." The list of new words to memorize seemed to get bigger every day, as did my feeling of being overwhelmed.

I spent too much time in my room, staring into a mirror on the wall. I didn't recognize myself in oxford shoes instead of sneakers, an ironed blouse instead of a wrinkled T-shirt. Once, I put on a bindi and the same Indian bracelets I'd worn on my

Drake Rosemont interview. But I couldn't find myself in those, either. I flopped onto the bed, grateful that at least I didn't have a roommate to see how pathetic I was. When I'd been home, all I'd wanted to do was escape. But now that I had, I was still trapped, somehow.

Within weeks, I began to walk differently, shoulders slumped, head down. While I made it to my classes and did my work, everything felt like a huge labor. It was impossible to make friends. I simply couldn't muster the courage to talk to new people. The girls all seemed worldly, confident, intimidating, and glamorous. And forget about the boys—they were clearly out of my league.

I longed for my sister and at times, to my horror, even my parents.

Just a month in, I was already toying with the idea of dropping out. Probably because I was always looking down, one day I noticed someone sprawled out on the grass of the quad. A girl. She was on her belly, her Drake Rosemont skirt bunched up around her butt and thighs. Underneath, she was wearing boxer shorts. The girl's head was propped in her hands. She watched the ground intently.

Her tomboy look gave me courage. I ventured a hello. It came out as a whisper.

When she didn't respond, I figured she hadn't heard me. Or that she was pretending not to hear.

"Hi yourself," she said, just as my resolve disintegrated completely.

I recognized her voice. She was in my biology class. We had something in common, something I could glom on to.

"You have Branston, right? I think I'm in your Tuesday morning seminar. What do you think of him?" I asked.

Still, the girl didn't turn to me. "He's all right. Nothing special."

I tended to agree. With mutton chop sideburns and a stuffed aardvark in the corner of his classroom, Branston was eccentric enough to impress us. He gave off an air of weirdness and intrigue. Unfortunately, it was clear after only a few classes that he was unremarkable. His teaching stirred nothing in our hearts.

"What did you think of class today?" I persisted.

She looked up for the first time. I liked her sturdy gaze and pink cheeks. A pimple studded her chin. Unlike most of my female classmates, she wasn't wearing makeup.

She shrugged noncommittally, then patted the grass beside her. "Come on. Have a look."

Kneeling beside her, careful to keep my skirt in place, I wondered if I was making a mistake. I was depressed, but I wasn't desperate. Not yet.

"I'm Sam, by the way," I told her.

"Mel," she replied.

What she showed me were ants. Lots of them. Black ants in a procession. Black ants running scattershot. Some carried bits of something jellied and white. There were also red ants. These, fewer in number, appeared to be losing a battle with the black ants.

"Why are they fighting?" I asked.

"It could be over territory. Or food. Or pheromones."

"Pheromones?"

"They're like smells. Each ant colony uses different pheromones to recognize each other."

"They're killing each other over how they smell?"

"People have killed each other over less."

Mel gave me a little magnifying glass and pointed to one of
the black ants. "See the tiny prongs at the front end of her body?
Those are jaws. They're called mandibles. She's gonna use them
to bite that red ant."

Peering through the glass, I asked, "How do you know
it's a girl?"

"The females do all the fighting."

"What do the males do?"

"Not much. Mating mostly."

Though it was autumn and too cold to be lying on the
ground, Mel and I stayed put for a long time. The more I stared
at the ants, the more fascinated I became. I felt as if I were
watching an epic story in miniature.

"Who knew ants could be so interesting," I told her, still
peering through the magnifying glass.

Mel motioned with one hand to our classmates, who scurried along the flagstone walkways. A few of them glanced at us
curiously. "A war is happening and none of them know it. They
never step off the path. They never *see*."

Then and there, I decided I liked Mel. She was an original, a person utterly and remarkably herself. I doubted she'd ever wasted a whole hour trying to find herself in a mirror.

"When we're done, do you wanna grab lunch?" I asked.

"I'm meeting my sisters in the dining hall at one. What time's it now?"

I glanced at my cell phone. "Twelve thirty."

"Why don't we stay conscientious objectors for a little longer, then meet them together?"

"No, it's okay. I don't want to mess up your plans." I was beginning to feel nervous again.

"You won't mess anything up."

"You sure?"

"Yeah. I spend too much time with my sisters anyway."

Suddenly, a pair of heels stopped inches from my head. Some of the teachers wore heels, but not like these: pink, strappy, expensive-looking. Immediately, I knew whom they belonged to. There was only one student at Drake Rosemont who could get away with wearing shoes like that.

Rittika Singh.

I looked up, awestruck.

"What are you doing?" she asked condescendingly.

"A little entomological study," Mel said.

"A little *what?*"

"I lost my contact lens," I said. "Mel's helping me look for it."

"Oh," she replied, a little disappointed. "I just stopped by to say, Mel, you really ought to invest in some new underwear."

When she walked away, I expected Mel to be embarrassed,

but she wasn't ruffled at all. Instead, she looked at me with new interest—like I was an interesting specimen worthy of further study. I figured she was surprised by how I'd handled Rittika.

That lunch with Mel turned out to be the first of many. Soon, I was eating most of my meals with her, and with her sisters, too. Soon I was inseparable from her, out of loneliness and even clinginess at first, and then because there was no one else I'd rather spend my time with. By the end of my first semester, I was no longer depressed. I had a new best friend. My first best friend, outside of my sister, Alexa.

I'm not sure when it happened, exactly, when Mel and her sisters started to feel more like family than my own family did, when I started to feel like I belonged with them, a half-Indian adoptee among wild blond Amazons. But it did happen. At night, at the edge of sleep, I liked to imagine what Mel and I would do after Drake Rosemont. We'd go to the same college, naturally. And when we graduated, we'd live together in New York City, in Brooklyn, probably. Mel, her sisters, and I would share a huge, drafty loft. We'd eat cereal together in the mornings, drink tea that had been grown in Mrs. Sharpe's greenhouse, and divide the rent six ways. Mel and her sisters would be scientists, veterinarians, anthropology professors, paleontologists, diplomats, or museum curators. As for my job, that was a little fuzzy. Truth be told, my own career plans were always the most vague. Funny how even in my own fantasies, I was a question mark to Mel's resolute period.

It took longer than we expected to locate the parachute. When we finally caught sight of it—its olive color barely distinguishable from the green canopy—we were covered in a new layer of sweat and mosquito bites. Mel craned her head as Pablo and Chester pointed high in the trees. From the ground, I couldn't make out what it was made of, but the fabric must have been thin. Every gust of wind caused it to billow and sway.

Chester appeared at Mel's side. "What's the plan, Captain?" he asked.

"Simple," she said. "We need to get it down. Think you can do it?"

It sounded like a dare. Taken aback, Chester raised his eyebrows. He wasn't used to being put on the spot.

"Sure," he said.

"Then show me."

He smiled. "Feeling feisty today, aren't we?"

Mel didn't respond. Every girl I knew loved to flirt with Chester, but Mel couldn't care less. She gave him her knife as well as instructions.

"Want me to come with you, bro?" Pablo asked.

Chester shook his head. "Naw, I got this."

"Sure?"

"Yeah, I'm sure."

Pablo looped his fingers into a stirrup and boosted Chester onto a branch. Slowly, hand over hand, Chester ascended the tree. He slipped a couple of times, and once, a branch broke clean off as he grabbed it, but he managed not to fall.

"Don't worry, man. You got this," Pablo called up.

The higher he climbed, the slower his progress. I caught him looking down a few times, and shuddered for him. If he fell at this point, he might not make it.

Close to the parachute, Chester clung for dear life and yelled, "The bark's grown *through* it." He was barely audible over the jungle's noisy backdrop. "I don't think I can get it down."

"You have to," Mel yelled back.

Rittika nudged her sharply with an elbow. "Why?" she demanded. "Is that old thing really worth it?"

"It might be."

Minutes passed. We watched Chester sawing and hacking with the knife. With every motion, I could sense Mel tensing up more. I seldom agreed with Rittika, but in this case I did: The parachute couldn't have been worth more than Chester's life.

Finally, he called, "Stand back, guys!"

He freed the bundle first. It swished through layers of understory, then landed on the mossy ground with a thud. It was larger than it had looked from the ground. Rish grabbed it and held it up.

"You can come back down now," he called to Chester. "Be careful."

"No—stay where you are," Mel yelled. "Get the parachute first."

"Mel!" I scolded.

But she didn't even look at me. She was too busy making sure Chester did as told. He did, crawling along branches that shouldn't have supported a person half his size, climbing, swinging, and cutting. The parachute was tangled widely—in multiple places in multiple trees. On the ground nobody spoke. Rittika bit her nails. Mel sucked her breath through her teeth.

Once or twice I remembered we weren't alone on the island and I looked around. But it was a mistake to worry about both Chester, whom I could see, and the enemy, whom I couldn't. My eyes darted, my heart pounded, my stomach went queasy. I felt the world spinning beyond my control.

Finally, Chester released the chute. For one glorious moment it sailed down, the fabric fluttering like a huge green butterfly. Then it snagged again on a lower rung of the understory. To his credit, he climbed down and began the process of untangling it all over again. This time, when he was finished, he wadded the chute into a ball and dropped it.

"Look out below," he yelled. When the wad reached the jungle floor, we cheered, overcome. Our voices rose even louder when Chester made it down, falling onto the balls of his feet, sweaty, red-faced, triumphant. He grinned and put out his hands. His palms were cracked and bleeding. His bare feet looked like they'd gone through a meat grinder.

"Good job!" Pablo said, high-fiving. Rish gave him that chest-bump hug that boys do. Chester smiled excitedly, then turned toward Mel expectantly. She stared at the blood trickling down his fingertips.

"Satisfied?" he asked.

"Don't wash in Conch Lake today," she replied. "You'll pollute it."

Chester stepped closer to her. He still had a huge smile on his face. "Can't I get a thank-you, Miss Get-the-Parachute-First?"

That smile could light up a stadium. Seriously. If I were Mel, I wouldn't have been able to resist it. But she sidestepped him and picked up the chute with both hands. She held it to her body, like a mother cradling an infant.

"Thank you," she said grudgingly. That was as much as Chester was going to get. But it was enough, I saw in my peripheral vision, to make Rittika frown.

"My guess is that it's from a war. Vietnam, the Korean War, maybe even World War Two," Mel said.

We returned to Camp Summerbliss to examine the parachute and open the tattered bundle, which had a white number and red cross on it. Mel guessed it was a paratrooper's kit, from one of Britain's airborne divisions.

Suddenly, her face got that look, that Mel look, like a kid on Christmas Eve, all sparkling eyes and hopeful wonder. "God, what if the enemy is actually an old paratrooper? Some poor soldier who got way off course and was stranded here. Or went AWOL."

"It's hard to imagine someone surviving years here, all alone," Betty said.

"But it's possible," Mel replied. She split the bundle with her knife and took the items out one by one. Betty, by her side, took inventory in a notebook. There wasn't much, and some of it wasn't even identifiable. She wrote,

5 Matchbooks (Rotted)

Compass (Waterlogged/Rusty)

Sewing Kit

Binoculars (Waterlogged)

1 Flare

Fishhooks and Fishing Line

3 Bottles Whiskey

First-Aid Kit

There were also some rusty cans and an even rustier can opener. At the bottom of the bundle, Mel produced some moldy shreds of fabric, which might have once been a blanket. I was surprised it hadn't disintegrated completely.

The sewing kit was in fair condition. The thread had somehow survived and might even be usable. The cans were not. Mel scratched the corroded metal with a fingernail. "These are decades past their expiration," she said. "And a botulism risk to boot."

"No gun? No knife?" Rittika said. "What was the point of getting all this down?"

"We don't know its value yet," Mel replied.

"Yes, we do. It's worthless. You risked Chester's life to get down a bunch of garbage."

"It's not all garbage," Betty argued, picking up the sewing kit. "Maybe we can clean the needles with sand. Get the rust off."

"Oh, goody," Rittika replied. "We can sew while the enemy hunts us down." Avery snorted in amusement.

"I didn't mean that we . . ." Betty said.

"Listen to me," Rittika said, cutting her off. "We humored Mel. Obviously, she was wrong, and the parachute wasn't worth it, but that's over with. It's time to focus on what matters: the enemy."

"Bringing him down," Rish added. Beside him, Chester nodded.

"Betty, write this down," Rittika instructed. "All the things we know about him so far. He uses a cane, right? And he knows English, at least a little—or else how did he write the note?"

"He steals shoes," Chester added ruefully.

"And crawls on girls!" Avery complained, shuddering.

"And he might be old—if Mel's theory's right," said Rish.

Maybe it was my imagination, but I didn't picture the enemy as an old soldier. I saw him as someone young, ruthless, and strong. Someone as much animal as man. Someone who had adapted to the jungle somehow, whose skin was immune to the incessant bites and the tireless sun, whose ears no longer thrummed from the constant shrieking of monkeys and birds, who didn't suffer the thirst, dread, and fatigue that plagued us Drake Rosemont kids. Basically, I pictured the enemy as invincible.

Which made us sitting ducks.

I glanced at Mel, wondering what she was thinking. It was hard to tell. Examining the parachute, she seemed lost in her own head.

Everyone began to gather around Rittika. Everybody except Anne Marie, who kept to herself. Rittika gave her the stink eye, then began handing out the swords. The rubber safety caps had been removed, exposing sharp steel tips. I pressed my finger against one, just shy of drawing blood. It wouldn't take a hell of a lot of pressure to hurt someone. I assumed the fencing position and lunged, the sword an extension of my arm. I bit my lip worriedly and almost drew blood there, too.

If we were back at Drake Rosemont, the idea of stabbing someone would be insane, outrageous, barbaric. But things were completely different here on the island. It was as if we were deciding the most basic things from scratch: what was good and bad, right and wrong. I didn't know if we were up to the task.

Because we were short of swords, Rittika demanded Mel's knife. She wanted to sharpen the ends of sticks to make spears. But Mel was reluctant.

We can't just go at this blindly," she said. "We need to make a plan."

"We have a plan," Rittika replied. "Find and kill—before we're killed first."

"But I'm not sure the enemy killed anybody."

Rittika put her hands on her hips. "Have you forgotten about Warren?"

"No—of course not. I just think there's a possibility he was already dead. Maybe the enemy used his body as a scare tactic."

"I doubt it. And besides, we can't just sit around, hoping for the best."

"All I'm saying is that we approach the hunt carefully. Prudently."

"*Prudently?* You sound like one of our teachers," Rittika scoffed. "I've got news for you—this ain't no Drake Rosemont."

"I don't want any of us to get hurt."

Rish interjected, "Man, I don't think we have that luxury."

"He's right," Rittika said. "Gimme the knife, Mel."

"We need to make some rules first."

"I'm not asking you. I'm telling you."

"Wait!" I said to Rittika. "Hear Mel out. We can spare a couple more minutes. Besides, what she has to say could save your skin."

I wasn't sure if that was true, but Mel glanced at me gratefully.

"Fine," Rittika said. I could tell by her voice I was skating on thin ice. "Let's hear it."

"First, we should go in pairs," Mel said slowly. "Stay close to your partner, no matter what. Second, be as inconspicuous as possible. Remember that the enemy knows this island better than we do. If you make noise or stand out, he'll see you way before you see him. And third, our goal isn't to kill him but to put him out of commission. We're not murderers."

That last word made me very nervous. I wasn't an aggressive person. I'd never even been in a fight before—no hair pulling, no slapping, nothing. The closest I'd ever gotten to one was a particularly vicious fencing bout in which my opponent had left bruises up and down my legs. Afterward, I'd examined them in a lavatory stall and cried.

"I think we can handle that," said Chester. "Don't you?" He looked at Rittika hopefully. She glared back, unwilling to be placated.

Finally, Mel handed her the knife. "I want it back when you're done," she said.

"You want a lot of things," Rittika snapped, taking the knife. She began gathering people to make spears. Meanwhile, I followed Mel to the edge of Conch Lake. I watched her peel up moss from the bank and scoop up loamy, brown-black soil. She began to smear it on her skin—her legs and arms first, then her neck and face.

"I'm not sure I want to know what you're doing," I told her.

"Trying to pass as Indian."

"What?"

"It was a joke."

"Oh."

"Mud offers good protection against sun and mosquitoes. Aboriginal Tasmanians have used it for centuries."

"I guess they aren't vain."

She shook her head, but I could see a hint of a smile. Her pale eyes looked bigger than usual in her mud-streaked face.

"Hey, do you think the others listened to me?" she asked.

"Yes, I do."

"Rittika doesn't know what she's doing."

I shrugged. "Do any of us?"

Mel shook her head. "I guess you have a point. You know, you should apply this, too."

"Thanks, but I'll risk a few more bites."

"Do you wanna risk malaria, Zika, yellow fever, dengue, encephalitis, and filariasis?"

I didn't know what half of those were, but they sounded bad enough for me to swallow my pride. Soon I'd spread mud just about everywhere. It felt cool and pleasant at first, but then hardened into a dry, dusty paste.

When the spears were finished, Rittika gave the knife back to Mel. Then she began to assign partners. I wondered if Mel was bothered by the way she had taken control. Rittika paired herself with Rish, Pablo with me, Chester with Ming, and Mel with Anne Marie. I wasn't surprised when she put Mel and Anne Marie together. Rittika didn't like either of them—Mel because she was smart, and Anne Marie because she was meek.

If there was one thing Rittika couldn't tolerate, it was weakness. I had a hunch that Rittika was a little jealous, too. Most students considered Anne Marie the best artist at Drake Rosemont. Every other month it seemed Drake Rosemont was showcasing some new installation or exhibit she'd put together. She received a lot of attention for her talent, from both staff and students. Rittika couldn't tolerate that, either—someone else in the spotlight.

She ordered the rest of the gang, Avery and Betty, to stay at Camp Summerbliss and keep the fire going.

Though a selfish part of me wanted to be with Mel, I didn't fight the pairings. It made sense, after all—to put the most able person with the most vulnerable. If push came to shove, Mel would do what had to be done. I had no doubt about that— especially after seeing how decisively she'd cut the boar.

As for me, well, I didn't want to consider my chances.

When it was time to go, Rittika came over and looked me up and down in amusement. I thought about jumping into Conch Lake and washing off the mud. Even here, a million miles from Drake Rosemont, I still wanted to look cool. I still wanted her approval.

"No need to worry, Samantha," she joked. "Your skin's already the right color."

"Mel said the mud keeps mosquitoes away," I stammered.

"Do you believe her?"

"She's usually right."

"Not about everything."

I looked down, feeling defensive, but not wanting to show it. I didn't want Rittika to know which side I was on.

"Have you noticed," she began, "that some of us are thriving on this island, while others"—she nodded in the direction of Mel—"aren't?"

"What do you mean?"

"Just look at them," she continued, glancing now at Anne Marie. "They're so white, their skin is literally frying!"

"It's not their fault. The sun's brutal here."

"It's not their fault, but it still sucks. They can't adapt like we can."

"What do you mean?"

"We're naturally stronger, Sam. Me, you, Rish. Pablo, too. And it's not just our skin I'm talking about. Darker people in general—we're survivors. We've always been survivors. Unlike the *Pales* over there."

"I don't get what you're saying," I replied, although maybe I just didn't want to get it.

"It's simple, if you think about it. Whiteness is like nature's warning sign. The paler the person, the more damaged they are. Not that it's the Pales' fault—and not all of them, of course."

"That sounds kind of . . . racist."

"Maybe it is," she sniffed. "But you've gotta admit there's something to it. Take Anne Marie. I honestly pity her. She's the ultimate Pale. I mean, have you ever met a less stable person? At Drake Rosemont she's bad enough—I can't tell you how many times I've tried to talk to her and ended up scaring her away. But here? It's ten times worse. Everyone walks on eggshells around her. God forbid we *hurt her feelings*." She sighed disgustedly.

"I don't know . . ."

"Look, it's no secret: The Pales have tried to keep us down since the beginning of history. But we always rise up. At some point we'll seize the power."

I wasn't sure how much of Rittika's sermon to believe. I wasn't even sure how much she believed. All I knew was that when I thought about Mel, I felt guilty.

"So if they're the Pales, what are we?" I whispered.

She laughed. "Let's see . . . Oh, I got it, the *Golds*." She waved her hand across the air, as if showing me a headline.

"Those are the official names: the Golds and the Pales?"

"That's right. We're mortal enemies, like the Montagues and the Capulets, the Greasers and the Socs, the Sharks and the Jets."

Against my better judgment, I laughed, too. Rittika seldom bothered talking to me. I couldn't deny that it felt good to have her attention. To be included.

"So, do you think we'll get this guy?" she asked, switching the subject.

"Do you?"

"My brother says we have a good shot."

"I don't know—I'm . . . a little scared."

"I am, too. But something about this island makes me feel like I could do anything."

"Not me. I'm the opposite. I just wanna get home," I admitted.

"Why?" she demanded. "Everything at Drake Rosemont is so boring. Every day's a routine. There's no mystery. It's almost like my life is already written out: graduation, then college, then I'll start working at my father's company. With Rish, of course."

"I thought you wanted to work at your father's company."

"Not really. But it's gonna happen. It's been my destiny since—like—forever."

"What do you really want to do?"

"I don't know—something creative. Acting, maybe. I just wish I had time to decide. To try things."

"Maybe you should tell your dad that."

She rolled her eyes. "Oh, come on, Sam. You know he'd go nuts. You have an Indian father, too!"

I blushed so deeply that I was actually grateful for the mud on my face.

"What does your father want *you* to do?" she asked.

"Me? My dad and I don't talk much. We're not close."

While she took this in, she slapped a mosquito that had landed on her thigh. A breeze blew and I caught a whiff of her hair. It smelled perfumy. I wondered if she had a secret shampoo stash, or if everything about her was just preternaturally perfect.

Truth was, I had always been fascinated by Rittika's hair. The obsession had started the first time I'd ever sat behind her in class. I spent a disproportionate amount of time ignoring the professor and staring at those lush locks. Once, I'd even picked up a stray strand from her back and wound it around my finger. The whole class had been taking notes, typing furiously on laptops, but I'd missed everything the professor had said. I'd worn the hair all day long, twined around my finger like a ring.

"Well, be glad you got your father's skin at least," she said. "We're gold—the real thing. Mel, with her mud—she's just a poor imitation."

Nervously, I giggled along with her. Then I glanced at Mel, to make sure she hadn't heard.

EIGHT

AT THE LAST MINUTE, MEL HANDED ME HER KNIFE. I didn't want to take it, but she insisted.

"Don't worry, I have a spear," she said. "And I know how to use it."

I believed her.

"Remember," she continued, "keep your eyes peeled, and come back early. Don't stay in the jungle at night." She looked me in the eye. "You'll be okay."

We hugged, then I joined Pablo and set off.

As we tromped over greenery and vines, I caught him staring at me sideways. I touched my encrusted cheek uncomfortably.

"What?" I demanded.

"Nothing. It's just you look very glamorous."

I shoved him playfully.

"Seriously," he continued. "It's a good idea—the mud. Good protection."

"I guess. Hey, Rittika said something interesting to me—that on the island, brown people have the advantage."

"The advantage? Like how?"

"I don't know—like, how we're superior because we're darker."

"Yeah, she would say that. It's basically the opposite of white supremacy, but just as screwed up. Rittika has a unique way of looking at the world. That's what comes from having the world's richest dad."

"She seems pretty confident we'll find the enemy."

"Confidence is good, but overconfidence isn't. I'm with Mel—we should have prepared better."

"You don't think we can do this?"

"We're not hunters! I don't even like to step on bugs."

I liked the way Pablo didn't try to impress me or make himself out to be something that he wasn't.

"I hope we don't see him—the enemy," I said.

"Yeah, you're not the only one."

"But if we do . . ."

"We have to put him out of commission," he replied grimly.

"How are we going to do that?"

"You're the one with the knife."

"But I don't know if I can use it."

At that, he stopped and looked at me squarely. "Look, even though I'm scared out of my mind, I'm still gonna use this spear if I have to." I glanced at the sharpened stick in his hands. "You gotta be ready, too."

I nodded and we continued walking in the direction Rittika had chosen for us. We were to survey a southwest swath of the jungle. As we walked side by side, I was aware of his elbow brushing my arm, of the synchronicity of our breathing. I was equally aware of the density of the jungle, of the nearly impenetrable green. Even if I lived here for twenty years, I wouldn't get used to the riot of trees, vines, and shoots. All of them were cross-hatched, pressing over, under, across, and between.

Keep your eyes peeled, Mel had warned.

But it was impossible. I closed my eyes every few moments just to let them rest. A headache was building behind my temples like the one I'd had right after the crash. There was just too much to take in. The green color wheel was spinning out of control. The enemy could be hiding anywhere: on a bower overhead, in the thicket to the right, under the curtain of ivy to the left, behind the mossy bank we'd just passed. Every creak, crack, and snap startled me. Every rustle and drip made me tremble.

I jumped when Pablo took hold of my arm.

"What?" I whispered urgently.

"Relax."

"What?"

"You stopped breathing."

"No, I didn't."

"Yes, you did."

With his spear he started swatting at the brush ahead of us. I concentrated on that motion: the whipping of the sharpened cane back and forth, back and forth. I concentrated and tried to remember to breathe.

I kept my knife in the air, like Pablo kept his spear. We walked in concentric circles, or what we thought were concentric circles. It was hard to know precisely where we were or where we'd been, even though we noted landmarks, the location of the sun, everything Mel had told us. We saw butterflies, birds, snakes, frogs, monkeys, lizards, the flash of something four-legged and yellow disappearing in the distance. I swore it was a jaguar. It was more likely a figment of my reeling imagination.

The tension didn't abate. I grew more tired by the minute. I started to understand how people were able to sleep amid warfare, in the most uncomfortable of places, in the most treacherous of conditions. It must come upon them, the sleep, like a torrent. It was impossible to stay hyperalert like this without the body and mind giving out.

Pablo and I walked and searched for hours. He noticed before I did how the sun was falling, how the shadows were growing longer. I didn't know why, but I felt closer to him than ever before. I trusted him. When we decided to go back to camp, we began to talk. We spoke quietly and intensely, still on guard but not quite as wary.

"Tell me the story of how you got to Drake Rosemont," he said, his eyes focused on the jungle. "Were you recruited?"

"Me? What for? No."

"For being mixed."

"You mean half Indian?"

"Yeah."

"Do they recruit for that?" I asked, remembering something Alexa had once told me.

"Well, not exactly. But they do like diversity—especially URMs."

"What's a URM?"

"Under-Represented Minority. I bet you got counted as one and didn't even know it. Who was your Drake Rosemont interviewer—Mrs. Duval?"

"Yeah. You had her, too?"

"Yup. She was ecstatic that I'm half Mexican. I guess they needed me to meet some quota."

"Really?"

"Oh, yeah. I'm pretty sure some of their funding depends on getting students of color."

"Students of color—I hate that. What does it even mean?"

"I know—seriously, right? Like if you're some shade other than white, you're suddenly riding a rainbow."

"I don't even know if I consider myself a *student of color.*"

"Well, you're a mixie, and Duval loves mixies. We're brown enough to be considered minorities, but white enough not to make anyone uncomfortable."

"Did you just call us *mixies?*"

"Yeah, mixies! Mixed race—you and me, kid. We're the hot new thing."

"I guess I should be flattered . . ."

"You know I'm being sarcastic."

"Yeah, I get that. So are there other mixies, besides you and me?"

"Sure. Lots of people. Ming, Chester . . ."

"Chester?!"

"Yeah, he's part Native American. Like, one-sixteenth or something like that."

"I never would have guessed."

"No joke. That kid looks like a Nordic Viking—like a teenage Thor."

I giggled. And I realized something. Pablo was funny—and fun to be around. He wasn't typical crush material, but he was a lot more interesting. I was surprised that I hadn't noticed before.

"Hey, can I ask you something?" he said.

My heart skipped a beat. "Sure."

"Do you like it here?"

"What do you mean?"

"Being on the island—do you like it?"

"I don't know. All I've thought about since being here is getting off—and getting away from the psycho who's threatening us."

"I'm the opposite! All I can think about is staying. This is my definition of paradise. I can't believe there isn't some big, fancy resort here. I can't believe some developer hasn't come with his crew and torn down the trees to put in a golf course and casino and whatever other crap developers put up."

I laughed.

"Sorry," he said shaking his head. "I'm a little cynical."

"Aren't you too young to be cynical?"

He looked at me ruefully. "Probably. Chester won't even talk to me about environmental stuff anymore. He says I'm obsessed. But I think the way I feel is a logical response to our planet going down the toilet."

We were silent for a few minutes, then Pablo said, "Hey, you want to see something crazy?"

I shrugged, not sure what to expect. "Okay—I think . . ."

Pablo smiled and turned. He'd ripped his Drake Rosemont trousers into shorts. Now he dropped them low enough for me to see a small black tattoo above his butt. It looked kind of like a cat, but was so sloppy and misshapen, it was hard to tell.

"Oh my . . ."

"What? You don't like it?"

"I want to tell you it's not terrible, but I'd be lying."

"Now, that's cruel, Samantha."

"Sorry!" I laughed when he pretended to look hurt.

"My friend from home inked it on me and two other guys. He'd never tattooed anyone before. We were his guinea pigs."

"But why a cat? And why your *ass*?"

"It seemed like a good idea at the time. And it's not a regular cat. It's an Iberian lynx. They're close to extinction. There are only, like, a hundred left."

"That's terrible."

"Yeah—it is. I got the tattoo to remind myself about conservation."

"For me, your tattoo's more like proof."

"Proof?"

"Proof that tattoos are always a bad idea!"

"All right, all right. Calm down," he joked.

"Well, now I know your deepest, darkest secret."

He smiled, and I thought for the first time that his smile just might rival Chester's. "Yeah, I guess you do."

NINE

PABLO AND I MADE IT BACK TO CAMP SAFE AND
sound. We were the last ones back. Immediately, I could see
something else had gone wrong. Mel's brow was furrowed. The
camp was buzzing with news: Anne Marie had gotten hurt.

Mel explained what had gone down. She and Anne Marie
had explored the caves but hadn't found anything. On their way
back, Anne Marie had fallen through a clump of palm fronds,
straight into a hole in the ground.

"It was definitely man-made," Mel said. "It was about eight
feet deep, and totally disguised on the jungle floor. All Anne
Marie did was take one wrong step. The ground gave way and
she tumbled down." She shook her head. "It was a trapping pit."

"What's that?" I asked.

"It's a classic hunting trap. They've been around since the
Stone Age. All I can think about is what would have happened if
she'd been alone. She hurt her leg pretty bad. It's not broken, but
it's banged up. She wouldn't have been able to climb out. She
could have been stuck there for days. She could have *died*."

"Well, that didn't happen," I said, hoping to make her feel
better. I could tell she was shaken.

"Was anything in there?" Pablo asked.

"Yeah, some old bones," she replied. "Animal bones."

"What about people bones?" Chester asked.

"No—no human bones."

"Was the trap meant for people?" I asked, feeling goose bumps rise on my skin.

"It's hard to say. Trapping pits are usually for animals. They get trapped inside, and then they're killed—for food, or trophies." Mel paused, lost in thought. "But I can't rule out that it was meant for us."

"You think the enemy made it?" Chester said.

She shook her head. "I just don't know."

"Where is Anne Marie now?" I asked.

"She's resting in the tent. She's pretty freaked out."

"No wonder."

"She doesn't want to see anyone."

"I'm gonna go anyway," I said, surprising myself.

Night was falling and the air inside the tent Betty had woven was murky and thick. I could barely make out the outline of Anne Marie's body, curved like a comma on the ground.

"Can I come in?" I whispered.

When she didn't say anything, I crawled inside and sat cross-legged beside her on the bare ground, the top of my head skimming the pitch of the roof. As my eyes adjusted to the darkness, I got a fix on Anne Marie's face. Her eyes were wide open.

"I heard what happened," I said. "I'm sorry."

"Don't be sorry. It wasn't anyone's fault—except for the person who made that trap."

Her voice sounded flat and exhausted.

"How's your leg?"

"I'm trying not to think about it. I'm trying not to think about anything."

I got the sense that she still wanted to be alone. It wasn't as if Anne Marie and I were good friends or anything. We had a few classes together, and of course we were both on the fencing team, but we didn't talk much, and when we did, it was almost always about assignments or our fencing schedule. Polite conversation.

I didn't want to leave, though. I liked Anne Marie—she'd always struck me as special. Maybe it was the fact that I'd seen so much of her art—paintings, sculptures, and photographs—and it had made an impression on me. Obviously, it had made an impression on other people, too, because a few galleries showcased her work and private collectors commissioned it. Once or twice I'd browsed her website. I didn't get the meaning behind a lot of her stuff, but there was no denying her ability to make big statements and grab attention. Her huge watercolors of flowers were especially arresting: pansies, daisies, columbine, and violets blown up larger than life, on canvases six, eight, even ten feet tall.

Being so quiet, Anne Marie clearly expressed herself best through her art.

She touched a large bump, like a golf ball, on her shin. "It's really hot. I don't know why."

"Your body is sending extra cells to repair the injury. All that cellular activity is generating warmth."

"Oh," she replied, surprised. "Are you going to be a doctor or something?"

"No. I just know that from Mel. I know all kinds of random stuff from her."

She smiled, but it was a rueful kind of smile. "In a weird way, it's good to have this to concentrate on. I've felt pretty out of it since the crash."

"I think all of us have."

"Yeah, but it's a little different for me. I don't have my meds with me."

I felt relieved and nervous at the same time: relieved that she was sharing; nervous that she might be in real trouble.

"What happens if you don't take them?"

"I guess the best way to put it is—I have a hard time figuring out what's real and what's not. The world, like, loses its structure."

"Have you ever been off your meds before?"

"Yeah, and it didn't go well. So to get off like this—cold turkey—it sucks."

"Just try not to worry, okay? I'm sure we'll be rescued soon. Who knows—maybe even tonight. You just have to hold on."

"Yeah, but what if we're here for weeks? Did you ever watch

that old show—*Gilligan's Island*? How long were those poor suckers stranded?"

Despite her earnestness, I cracked up. "I *wish* this was like *Gilligan's Island*. To me, it's more like *The Hunger Games*."

"True," she replied, rubbing her bruise.

"How long will it be before you start feeling . . . the effects?"

"Oh, I'm already feeling them."

"Is there anything I can do?"

"Find me a pharmacy?"

I reached for her hand and squeezed it. It was tiny, like a child's hand.

"Anne Marie, we're going to be fine."

"I don't know. I don't know if we will. But . . . it means a lot that you came to talk to me."

"Oh—come on. Don't be ridiculous."

"I'm not being ridiculous. Not everyone cares, not everyone's like you."

Instantly, I thought of Rittika. To her, Anne Marie was probably more of a hindrance than anything else. What had she called her? *The ultimate Pale.* I forced a smile and hoped my discomfort didn't show. I was treading unfamiliar territory here. Heart-to-hearts weren't my thing. My family never had them, except the times Alexa and I broke down about our parents' dysfunctional marriage. Most of my intimate conversations were with Mel, who wasn't a particularly emotional person either. I wasn't used to opening up or being someone's sounding board.

Not surprisingly, a part of me wanted to flee the tent at that moment. But I didn't. Even if it meant leaving my comfort zone, I wanted to be Anne Marie's friend. I wanted to help her. She looked so skinny and small and weak. To be honest, she reminded me of my sister.

"Listen," I said. "You should try to sleep—it's late. Tomorrow will be a better day."

"You promise?"

"I promise," I said, smiling. But we both knew it was a promise I couldn't necessarily keep.

Later on, after my shift had ended, I tried to get some sleep. But every time I closed my eyes, Warren would appear. I couldn't get the image of him on the beach out of my head. Time and again, I saw his blank eyes. I smelled his putrid, decaying odor. The more I tried to forget him, the more stubbornly he returned. Without my consent, my imagination added gory details: snails sucking on his skin, seabirds picking him apart, hermit crabs crawling through his rotting guts.

The only way to forget him for good was to think about something almost as disturbing—the fact that the fake eye had disappeared. Mel told me it was gone from the forked tree. Like Chester's shoes, it had simply vanished. Maybe there was a logical explanation for its absence. Maybe a strong gust of wind had dislodged it and it had rolled away. Maybe an animal had managed to move it. I came up with a bunch of possible explanations, but I didn't believe any of them.

What I did believe, deep inside, was that the eye was still

watching us, somehow. Still seeing everything we were doing. I sat up and looked all around, trying to gaze beyond the glowing fringes of the campfire, all the way into the pitch black of the jungle. But of course I couldn't, and it was with a sense of failure that I finally fell asleep.

The next day, more paranoid than ever, we continued to search the island. We went over the same ground again, retracing our old steps, worried on top of everything else about traps in the earth. Just as yesterday, we came away with nothing to show for it. The day after that was the same. A sense of futility began to descend upon us. The more we searched, the more elusive the enemy seemed.

"He could be anywhere," Mel said. "There's no way to really comb this place. We'd have to burn it down."

She was right. Even if we went over the island a thousand times, the enemy could still evade us. All he had to do was move around from one overgrown, leafy hideaway to the next. It would be easy. Child's play. Yet frequently, I got an icy sensation, the feeling that he was nearby, right over my shoulder, watching everything we were doing.

Mel was convinced he spent at least some time in the caves. "It's the best natural shelter on the island," she told me. "The only reason *we're* not there is because our fresh water is here, near Conch Lake."

"But you searched the caves, and didn't see him."

"Maybe he knew we were there and hid."

Several more times she returned to the caves. She took different partners—me, Chester, Pablo, even Rish. Mel made torches so we could see through the darkness. She drew a detailed map of the interior. The caves were more extensive than we'd thought, and included at least a dozen detours and dead ends. Still, we never found any sign of the person who had written the note on the sand or dug the trap that had hurt Anne Marie. We never found any sign of anyone.

When Mel made seven tallies on the forked tree—a full week on the island—we finally admitted aloud what we were all feeling: We wouldn't find the enemy until he wanted to be found.

We stopped looking. We stayed closer to Camp Summerbliss and kept the fire burning. We wrote in giant letters along the beach MAYDAY and SOS in case a plane flew overhead. Each of us had daily chores. Like Betty said, it was better to stay busy. When we were idle, it was easy to fixate on the enemy. To imagine what he might do.

Avery foraged for fruit. On the beach, she collected seaweed, which was surprisingly tasty when washed in freshwater and dried in the sun. Ming assumed the role of cook. She dove for most of the conch, removed the meat from their shells, and cleaned it. She kept us from getting tired of the same old food by whipping up new recipes: conch and fruit salad, conch wrapped in banana leaves, conch soup with seaweed in halved coconut shells.

Mel was in charge of keeping us hydrated. After several false starts, she'd found a way to store water. In the jungle, she'd happened across wild gourds, which she'd picked and laid on the beach. On the sun-scorched sand, the gourds dried up in no time. Their green stripes faded to brown. Their skins turned parched as baked clay. Mel cut off the tops with her knife and emptied out the guts. When cleaned, each of the gourds could hold several pints of freshwater. Betty tied handmade string around the waists of their pear shape. We wore the gourds like canteens around our necks.

Impressed, I asked Mel where she'd learned to make them. "From some remote indigenous tribe your father met?"

"No. From *The Swiss Family Robinson*," she replied.

As her leg healed, Anne Marie spent most of her time on the far side of the island, the part Mel identified as the "tail end." She liked to sit on the outcrop, which was like a natural lookout tower, and stare at the ocean. I was worried about her being all alone and far away. But Mel was happy someone was stationed there, should a ship sail by. Mel had shown Anne Marie how to build a fire and make smoke signals, but when I visited her at the lookout tower, the fire was always out.

I worried that her lack of medication was taking a major toll on her health. She was even more detached lately, her eyes dreamy, her thoughts locked away. When I visited her, I tried to draw her out a little. But she wasn't as open as she'd been that night in the tent. While I tried to make conversation, she would just watch the lapping waves, as mesmerized as she'd been when

I'd caught her staring into the jungle. And when she did speak, it wasn't in response to what I was saying. She complained, instead, about tricks the clouds were playing on her eyes. How they were conspiring with the waves to make a submarine bobbing in the water, or a giant ocean liner, or a fleet of white sailboats.

"Mirages," she said. "There for a few seconds, then lost."

That was the same way I was beginning to feel about her.

The boys kept watch over Camp Summerbliss, patrolling. But at least once a day they went fishing. Though they were scared of sharks, they loved to swim in the shallows inside the reef. Using fencing swords, they tried to spear any fish that looked edible. If that didn't work, they used the fishhooks or dragged for fish with a net Betty wove for them. Whenever they caught something, they returned giddy and charged up. We would roast succulent white fish or speckled crabs and have a feast.

Rittika occupied herself with beachcombing. She looked for shells, coral, and sea glass. But she also sorted through the garbage that washed up on our island. I secretly found this amusing. At Drake Rosemont, Rittika would have scoffed at anyone touching trash. But here, she had no issues—maybe because trash was one of the few visible reminders of our past. On her outings, she usually found plastic water bottles. She also found straws, milk jugs, soda cans and rings, unraveling pieces of rope, cigarette filters, garbage bags, even condoms and syringes. All that trash—it was disgusting. It made me realize that Pablo was right to be worried about the state of our planet.

As for Betty, she was the most industrious of all of us. She wove more tents, as well as baskets, sun hats, mats, even a hammock. The supplies tent was one of her most useful creations. Rittika put the water bottles and other assorted odds and ends from the beach inside the tent. We also stowed the items from the parachute there, as well as the contents of our backpacks and pockets: books, pens, a deck of cards, wallets, pocket change, and dead cell phones.

More days passed. I realized something when I woke up in the new tent I shared with Mel, watching bits of light dancing through the weft. It felt almost normal to be here. Roles had been more or less established. Life had already taken on a certain rhythm, a certain beat.

But this life wasn't anything like the one we'd led at Drake Rosemont. In fact, we were even beginning to look different. Gone were the sleeves and collars of our school uniforms. We wore as little fabric as possible to stay cool in the island heat. The Pales turned pink, the Golds ever darker.

Free of Drake Rosemont's restrictions, the girls wore their hair wild and tangled. We put on jewelry we'd made ourselves: necklaces, earrings, and bracelets constructed from cowrie shells, abalone, coral, feathers, and mother-of-pearl. Betty made a whole necklace from chips of white and blue china she'd found in a tidal pool. She wondered aloud if they'd been part of an old English tea set. Pablo retorted that they were probably remnants of a dollar-store plate made in China, washed out to sea by sewage runoff.

Rittika rubbed her teeth with crushed shells until they turned blindingly white, especially against her dark skin. We followed her lead, as we always did. Our smiles gleamed lupine and dangerous. I didn't want to admit it, but I liked the animal look of myself in the reflection of Conch Lake.

As for the boys, they looked different, too. The khaki fabric of their torn shorts had faded from sunlight and salt water. Waistbands slung low on their hips, revealing pelvic bones, happy trails, waists made leaner from our Spartan diet. At Drake Rosemont, I wouldn't have stared at their new bodies. Now I did.

When we'd arrived on the island, we'd been neat, respectable, obedient, bland. Now we were creatures of our habitat—feral and unpredictable. It seemed to me only Mel remained the same. Maybe that was because she was more resilient than the rest of us. Or maybe it was because Mel had been a child of nature long before we ever got here.

Another night, another girl screaming. I sat bolt upright and grabbed for Mel's hand. She wasn't there.

Terrified, I crawled out of the tent to a disconcerting sight. By the light of the fire, I saw Mel swatting and kicking at a swarm of monkeys. She bared her teeth, then leaned her head toward them aggressively, like a bull about to charge. They backed off for a few seconds, but soon began another attack.

There were a dozen of them—all near Anne Marie's tent, which was half-collapsed. And Anne Marie, she was the one who was screaming. She looked bleary-eyed and terrified, hopping from one foot to the next, trying to avoid one monkey's claws and teeth. She cried out as it scratched her still-tender leg in a fit of rage.

Betty and I locked eyes, then dashed toward the chaos. Imitating the monkeys, we yelled and jumped wildly. We'd hoped to scare them off, but our tactic only made them more enraged. One of the bigger ones came close and screeched maniacally, its eyes ablaze with frenzied wrath. The barbaric noise it made—that was the worst thing. Because it sounded so human.

Instinctively, I reached down, scooped up a handful of dirt, and threw it at the creature's face. Bull's-eye. With a yelp, it scampered away. Out of the corner of my eye, I saw pieces of food scattered around the edge of what remained of Anne Marie's tent. It dawned on me what must have happened: The monkeys had come for that food. In their enthusiasm, they'd knocked down Anne Marie's tent. They'd probably thought Anne Marie was their competition for the meal. Now they were defending their claim.

Waving swords and fists, Pablo and Chester came running. They tipped the balance in our favor. One by one, the other monkeys began to disperse, realizing they were outnumbered and overpowered. Two lingered, hissing at us, but when Mel hissed back, they slowly retreated into the jungle.

My heart was pounding so loud I wondered if everyone

around me could hear it. I'd never known monkeys could be like this—like demons.

"How did this happen?" Mel asked Anne Marie, who was huddled on the ground, whimpering. She looked smaller and more helpless than ever.

"I don't know," she sobbed. "I was in my tent. Sleeping. Then I started hearing noises. The next thing I knew, my tent came down, and there were monkeys everywhere."

"Why did you leave food near your tent?"

Anne Marie looked at the bits of conch and fruit still scattered nearby. "I didn't leave it. It wasn't there when I went to bed."

"So who the hell put it there?" Mel demanded, looking around.

"I did," Rittika said, out of nowhere. She came walking over, her face strangely serene. "It was for her own good. I thought it would help her."

"Why on earth would you think that?" asked Mel.

"You know perfectly well why, Mel. Tell me—when we were hunting the enemy, did you like having Anne Marie as your partner? It was like hauling bricks on your back, right? She's deadweight. And for some reason, everyone pretends that's okay. It's not. She's gotta learn to stand on her own two feet. To protect herself. We've all got to do our share."

Mel shook her head. "I can't even believe what I'm hearing. It's crazy. You honestly think you were doing her a favor by siccing wild animals on her?"

"It's called tough love. I wanted her to see that she's capable of defending herself. I figured if she could fend off some animals, maybe there's hope for her. Otherwise, let's face it, she's just bait for the enemy."

Rittika looked at Anne Marie not unkindly. I couldn't swear on it, but I think she believed every word she said.

As her anger flared, Mel's red face turned even redder.

"Look at that," she demanded, motioning to Anne Marie's bleeding legs. "You are personally responsible for that. You made it happen."

"It didn't *have* to happen," Rittika insisted. "If she would have put up a fight, for once in her life."

"Monkeys, like all wild animals, are unpredictable. She could have died. Even now, she could have herpes B or rabies—thanks to you." As Mel scolded her, I knew she was also deliberating. Rittika had crossed a dangerous line. She'd taken someone else's life into her own hands. How she'd be judged for that was going to be up to us.

"She'll be fine," Rittika said, "because other people rescued her. *As usual.*"

"Give it a rest!" Pablo snapped. "What happened is simple—you put her life on the line. For no reason. And now you're criticizing her. Again for no reason. It's unforgivable."

"I'm just trying to make a point."

"Oh, really? If the same thing happened to you, you would have gone berserk! But things like that don't happen to people like you, do they? The walls of that ivory tower you live in must be pretty thick."

"Hey, back off, man," Rish said, stepping in.

"See what I mean?" Fiery-eyed, Pablo pointed at Rish, but looked at his sister. "No one is allowed to criticize you. Even when you almost kill someone. The least you could do is apologize."

"This has nothing to do with you," Rish said, blocking Pablo's chest with his hand. "Butt out."

"Hey, someone needs to teach her right from wrong. Clearly, she never learned it."

Rittika glanced from her brother to Pablo, and then back again. She looked unflustered, even amused.

"Forget about it, Rish. He's not worth it."

"I could say the same about you," Pablo spat.

Rittika ignored him. "Let's go. You too, Avery. Let's let the riffraff cool off."

Dutifully, Avery followed behind as they left. When they'd gone, Mel dipped a piece of torn cloth into Conch Lake. Pensively, she cleaned Anne Marie's scratches, then poured some whiskey from the parachute bundle over them. Anne Marie didn't complain. She didn't even flinch. She'd stopped crying, but I couldn't say she looked any better. Her face was expressionless—even catatonic.

Betty invited her to sleep the rest of the night in her tent. In the morning, she promised, she'd make Anne Marie a new one. Anne Marie nodded mutely. As she bent down to get inside, I watched her ridged backbone practically saw through her blouse. If she didn't eat more soon, she was going to turn into a skeleton.

I lay wide awake after that. The episode had fired me up. I felt angry at Rittika for her cruelty, and angry at Mel for not being able to stop it. But mainly I felt angry at myself because I hadn't done a thing. Talk about deadweight. With a sigh, I got up and tended to the fire.

At dawn, I was the only one still awake. One by one, my classmates crawled out of their tents to a new day. Nonchalantly, Rittika doffed her clothes and went for a swim in Conch Lake. Never mind that the boys were watching. She'd been comfortable with her body at Drake Rosemont, but here, she flaunted it. As if we didn't already see her superiority.

As for me, I waited for the boys to go patrolling before I bathed. I needed to feel the soothing weight of water. But even more important, I needed to gather my courage before speaking to Rittika.

In the water, she swam over to me and smiled brightly, as if last night had never happened. I wondered if she felt even remotely guilty, or if being Rittika meant never second-guessing yourself.

"Hi," she said, floating on the water.

"I want to talk to you," I told her.

"Okay, so talk."

"It wasn't right, what you did. Anne Marie is having trouble right now. She's kind of—sick."

"I think she has enough defenders, Sam."

"Anne Marie's different here. She's not like she was at school."

"Seriously—if she has a problem with me, *she* should talk to me."

"The thing is, I don't know if she can."

Effortlessly treading water, Rittika rolled her eyes. "I made my point last night. I'm sick and tired of hearing about what a fragile little snowflake she is. For once in her life, she needs to stand on her own two feet." Rittika looked me in the eye and shrugged. "I'm not trying to be a bitch. I'm just saying it like it is."

Without waiting for me to respond, she swam to the shore and climbed out onto the rocks. She sat there, face toward the rising sun, waiting for the early heat to dry her off. I scrabbled out after her, stubbing my toe and feeling more awkward than ever.

Still, I was determined not to let her off the hook. I sat beside her, wondering how to proceed. How do you teach someone compassion? Can you? In that silence, Rittika raised a finger and pointed at the birthmark on my shoulder. The blemish, the size of a fist, was a patch of hypopigmented skin—ivory white. Until I was eleven or twelve, I didn't care about it. But once I'd become more aware of my body, in the way teenagers do, I'd started to hate that birthmark. I thought twice about wearing tank tops or strapless dresses, fearing people would make fun of me. I got so self-conscious about it that I asked my mother if I could get it removed.

I figured she would be receptive. After all, looks were important to her. Superficial things were important. We hadn't had a real conversation in years, but my mom was always ready to discuss the state of my cuticles or whether I'd look good with bangs.

Yet when I'd asked her about the birthmark, she'd shaken her head.

"I don't want you to get rid of that," she'd said. "It's the only part of you that's like me!"

Maybe she'd been joking. But I was bothered by the comment. After that, I started to think of the birthmark as more than a blemish. It was a bona fide defect. Evidence of my mother's bad judgment. Evidence of my father's transgressions. Evidence of a mistake: two people who should never have gotten together, not because their skin didn't match or because they'd grown up on different continents, but because they had absolutely nothing in common. Nothing except the same two daughters.

Casually, Rittika ran her finger over the birthmark and pressed it like a button. Her touch felt hot and penetrating. I felt a shame so pure I wanted to cry.

"Why are you so self-conscious, Sam?" she asked. "Remember, you're better than that. You're *gold*."

TEN

THERE CAME A MOMENT WHEN WAITING DIDN'T MAKE sense anymore. I think we all felt it at the same time. Mel called a meeting. She had our attention. We were jumpy, uncertain, restless.

"Listen," she said, "until we contain the enemy, we have two options. Live with him, always on guard, always paranoid. Or get off the island."

We responded to this pronouncement with silence. I think most of us still believed rescuers would come. I think most of us couldn't believe they hadn't come already.

"It's up to us to rescue ourselves. We can't afford to wait any longer."

"You're being hasty," Rish replied. "There are people looking for us right this second. My father has access to an entire fleet of ships. I know he'll find us. He just needs more time."

"I'm sure *all* our parents are looking," Mel replied. "But that doesn't mean they'll find us. There are thousands of uninhabited islands in this world, and we seem to be on one of them."

"Mel's right," I said. "We need to be self-sufficient."

She nodded at me appreciatively. "Right. There's a big difference between waiting and doing."

Rittika frowned, but the rest of our classmates were willing to listen.

"We need to start by tapping into our creativity," Mel continued. "I want to show you guys an exercise my father once showed me. He wanted me to understand that sometimes all the tools you need are right in front of you."

Mel told us to spread out and find a little plot of ground. Each of us was to study a space the size of one cubic foot.

"What are we looking for?" Betty asked.

"We don't know. That's the point. Just find a little piece of ground that speaks to you."

We did as instructed, dispersing and claiming little plots within camp.

"Now look down," Mel said. "What do you see? Not much, right? But there's more here than you realize."

Mel had us cordon off our plots with sticks and vines. She told us to kneel down and study the area carefully. "Memorize every single thing you see. Every bug, plant, animal, blade of grass. Everything. Your plot might look small, but you'll be astounded by its biodiversity."

We obliged, compliant if bewildered. That lasted about five minutes before Avery rubbed her neck and complained, "Why are we doing this again? It's boring."

"Don't let that fool you!" Mel said. "Boredom can be useful. Galileo made one of his most important discoveries while bored out of his mind. He was in church, watching a chandelier swaying above him. He started measuring the sways with his pulse.

He realized that time can be measured that way—by the swinging of a pendulum. We still use this principle today."

Avery looked unimpressed. "How old was he? Galileo? Thirty, at least. A lot older than us."

"He was twenty. Listen, we're not too young to do important things. In fact, being young is a bonus. Young minds aren't constrained like old ones. Mozart composed some of his best work in his teens. Chopin, too."

Avery didn't appear moved by what Mel was saying, but I was. We might not be prodigies, but we had potential. And so did this island. We just had to open our eyes a little wider.

I left to get a pen and pad out of the supplies tent, then returned to my plot. I began to write down everything I could find in my cubic foot. I didn't know what to call most of the specimens—the purple-shelled beetle, the nubby-leafed plant, or the white butterfly that briefly flitted through—so I sketched and numbered each one. I was startled when I reached fifty and still wasn't done. I wouldn't have guessed so much life was crammed into so small a world.

Pablo, whose plot was nearby, saluted me playfully when I showed him what I'd written.

"What if something crawls into my space?" Betty asked. "A lizard just visited."

"He counts, too," Mel replied. "Notice how the plots are not static. They are constantly changing, full of surprises."

Rittika groaned in annoyance. She and Anne Marie were the only ones not participating. Anne Marie was lingering at the edge of camp, gazing into the jungle. Rittika was sunbathing on the ground in her underwear. After a while, she flipped onto her stomach and unsnapped her bra.

Ignoring her, Mel reminded us to be observant. When she stopped in front of my patch, I felt the dim of her shadow. "Look, Sam has already found fifty species. I bet she'll find a hundred if she looks hard enough. A hundred creatures—that's a whole universe of life."

"I still don't get the point of this," Avery muttered.

"The island, you could say, is our factory, our workshop. We have to understand all of the resources available here. If we know what we have to work with, we can devise a way home."

I looked around to see how the others were faring. Ming seemed to be enjoying herself, nose pressed to the ground, fingers busily searching. Betty was looking at my paper and pen, perhaps deciding whether to get her own. Anne Marie was still staring off into the jungle. Chester and Pablo, not surprisingly, were sneaking peaks at Rittika.

Mel continued to monitor us. She had piled her hair atop her head in a messy bun, stuck through with a twig. She wielded a long branch like a pointing stick. For a time, everyone was quiet. Then Ming mentioned that a tiny yellow frog had hopped into her plot.

Mel turned on her heels and dashed over to her. "Don't touch it," she warned.

"Why?"

"Did you touch it? The frog?"

"No."

"Let me see."

Ming pointed at the animal at the corner of her plot. It was as bright as a jewel, no bigger than a quarter.

"That's what I thought. A *Phyllobates terribilis*," Mel said.

"Elementary, my dear Watson, a *Phyllobates terribilis*," Rittika quipped, deepening her British accent.

Mel ignored her, continuing, "It's also called a poison dart frog. My father brought one back from Colombia once. When he touched it, he always wore gloves. If you have contact with it, you could die."

"I didn't touch it," Ming swore. All of us got up and gathered around Ming's plot. Even Rittika put on her bra and came over.

"Why is it called a poison *dart* frog?" I asked.

"Good question, Rockwell. The indigenous people of South America use the poison on the tips of blow darts. For hunting." Mel gazed at the frog admiringly. "It's an astonishing animal."

Astonishing or not, we kept our distance.

"*Phyllobates terribilis* come in a few colors—orange, green, white. But most are like this one: bright yellow, like gold," Mel continued. "The color's a warning sign to its enemies."

"I was already paranoid about where to walk," Ming said, bringing my mind back to the trapping pit. "Now it's going to be even worse."

We stood around Ming's plot until the frog hopped away and disappeared into a thicket. When Ming exhaled and knelt beside her plot again, we followed suit, but warily.

I was still roused by Mel's belief we could get ourselves off the island. But the poison dart frog had made me realize there might be more obstacles in our way, things we hadn't even imagined.

"Keep an eye out," Mel said. "He could be back."

I wasn't sure if she was talking about the frog or our enemy.

Later that same day, Mel and I notched off another mark in the tree. I had turned around to head back to Camp Summerbliss when she tugged my arm. "This way," she said. "I want to show you something." She put her finger to her lips. "Shh—don't tell anyone."

She led me deeper into the jungle. Following behind her, I saw that she was wearing her backpack. Beneath the riot of tangled tree limbs above, she found a small clearing on the jungle floor.

"Here's good," she said, stopping abruptly. She had a pensive, slightly disturbed look on her face. I watched her take off her backpack and sort through it. She took out a bamboo pole about a foot long. Holding the pole vertically, she shook it carefully and pulled out some moss from the top end. After she peered inside, she told me to have a look. There, sitting on a clump of moss at the bottom end of the hollow pole, was the little yellow frog. Mel quickly plugged the top end again so it couldn't jump out.

"Oh my god. How did you get it? Why did you get it?" Even though the frog was trapped inside the cane, I couldn't help panicking.

"I don't want to do what I'm about to do, but I feel like I have to. Spears and swords might not be enough," she said. She set the cane on the ground and searched nearby. It took her about a minute to find what she was looking for—a long, thin, straight twig. "Sorry, little guy," she whispered, taking the pole again. I watched her remove the pad of moss from the top and slide the twig into the cane.

"What are you doing?"

"Hurting it," she said simply.

"Why? Don't do that!"

"I have to. It could be a matter of *our* survival."

"Mel . . ."

"This little critter has enough poison in his body to kill ten people. Chances are," she said grimly, maneuvering the stick, "we'll need only enough for one."

I was repulsed by what she was doing. The last thing I wanted to know was how she was doing it, but she told me anyway. "I stuck the stick in his throat and out the back of his body. He's still alive, barely, and he's sweating poison. That's just what I need him to do."

"Oh god, that's revolting."

"The poison's white. Kind of frothy—like the foam on a cappuccino."

"Mel!"

"Here, hold this," she replied, handing me the cane. I held it as far away from my body as I could. She dug through her backpack again until she found a few syringes. "Thank you, Rittika," she said. "For once you were a help rather than a pain in the ass." She took the cane back and poked the stick inside until some of the poison stuck to the end. Then, ever so carefully, she scraped the poison into the syringes.

"Is that enough?" I asked her. There was only a drop or so in each one.

"Oh, yeah. It's potent stuff. My dad said it's stronger than cobra venom. If even a tiny bit enters the bloodstream, boom— you're dead."

She wrapped the syringes in several layers of leaves and put them back into her backpack.

"Where are you going to put that?" I asked.

"In the back of the supplies tent. I'll show you where, just in case."

We proceeded to dig a shallow grave for the frog. Covering up the bamboo cane with dirt, I wondered if we should say a prayer. But that would be ridiculous. After all, we'd never said one for Jeremiah, Warren, or the pilot. They hadn't even gotten a burial.

ELEVEN

SHORTLY AFTER THE CUBIC-FOOT EXERCISE, MEL ASKED the twins to take us to the tar pit. She was curious about it—and so were the rest of us.

Rittika was hesitant at first—she didn't see the point. But Rish talked her into it. And once Rittika agreed, everybody else jumped on the bandwagon. We proceeded in a snaky train, armed with our weapons, pushing through brush, stomping over vines. Though small, the tar pit wasn't hard to find. The stink was unmistakable—a trail that started out faint twenty yards away and became increasingly noxious the closer we got. At the edge of the pit, I gagged. The stench was worse than sewage, worse than diesel truck exhaust, almost worse than the smell of Warren's decomposing body. I wished I hadn't torn off the collar of my blouse. I wished I had something to press against my mouth and nose, anything to lessen the reek.

The smell was the only thing that gave the tar away. Coated with water and scattered with leaves, the pit looked like an ordinary pond. Mel knelt on the bank and dragged a stick through the black sludge beneath the water. When she pulled it out, sticky, stringy tar stretched from it like taffy. The sight of the tar was both exciting and disgusting. Chester and Rish found their own sticks and mimicked Mel. After a while they started to behave the way they had around the campfire the night they'd arrived. Like hoodlums. I watched them throw things into the pit: vines, branches, wadded-up leaves. These lay on the surface for a moment, then began a slow descent into oblivion. This is what must happen to animals, too, I realized, my stomach in knots.

I wondered how deep the pit was. Did the things that fell in, or were thrown in, travel ten feet down, twenty, all the way to the bowels of the earth? It was impossible to tell. The only thing I felt sure of was that they were gone forever. I didn't know how fossils were retrieved from La Brea Tar Pits, but I doubted anything could be fished out of this, our own private waste station.

As Chester and Rish continued to lob things into the pit, Rittika walked along the very edge. Avery urged her to step back, but her pleas only egged Rittika on. She smiled and pirouetted like a ballerina, her arms long and graceful above her head. I don't know why, but seeing her there, risking life and limb, I felt more envy than concern.

My attention switched back and forth between Rittika and the boys, who had hauled a huge branch out of the jungle. They swung it back and forth, gaining momentum. The queasy feeling in my stomach gained momentum, too.

"One. Two. Three!" they shouted euphorically, hurling the branch as far as they could. It landed with a colossal splash. Water droplets blasted into the air, then rained down. The tar swallowed the branch almost immediately, water rippling concentrically from the point of impact, then gradually going flat, as if nothing had happened.

Rittika laughed, pirouetted again, then dashed off to get her own branch. In silent collusion, Rish helped her drag it toward the pit.

"Step aside," Rittika snapped. She was talking to Anne Marie, who was standing in her way.

Everyone expected Anne Marie to oblige. So when she held her ground, we stared at her, bug-eyed.

"Please put that down," she told Rittika.

"What?"

"Don't throw it. We've already made too much noise."

"Oh-ho, look who finally put on her big-girl panties!" Rittika exclaimed, exchanging a titillated look with Rish.

"You don't understand—he might hear us." Panicked, Anne Marie turned 360 degrees as she scanned the jungle.

"Who might?" Rittika asked, setting down her side of the branch.

"The enemy—he's close. That's why you have to be quiet. The more noise you make, the more hungry he gets."

Rittika raised an eyebrow. I couldn't help but think that Anne Marie was doing exactly what she had wanted her to do. Stand up for herself. Make herself heard. Maybe the tough love had worked after all. But I don't think it had worked in the way Rittika had intended.

Head cocked to the side, she took a step toward Anne Marie. "How do you know he's around here?"

"I can feel him," Anne Marie whispered, stepping back in the direction of the pit. Again, she scanned the jungle urgently, attuned to an imminent danger only she could sense.

"I think you might be right," Rititka said, following the trajectory of her eyes. As if in a dance, she took another step forward, and Anne Marie another step back. "I think he's coming for us."

"Then let's go! What are we waiting for?"

"Where are we going to go, Anne Marie? There's no safe place. Not here."

Anne Marie got a pained look on her face. She raked her fingers through her dirty, snarled hair.

"I think he has his eye on you," Rittika continued. "He can sense weakness. He knows who's vulnerable. He's like a shark smelling blood in the water."

"Please," Anne Marie begged.

"Hey," shouted Pablo, "stop teasing her!"

Rittika continued to advance. "He knows the ones who are injured. The ones who can't get away."

Anne Marie's mouth twisted as she spat out a succession of nos, each one softer than the last.

"It doesn't matter what you say. If you don't watch out, he'll getcha!"

Suddenly, Rittika lurched forward, surprising Anne Marie,

who stumbled back roughly onto the narrow slope of the muddy bank. She tried to right herself but lost her balance and slid backward into the pit. Horrified, I watched her eyes widen in disbelief. She struggled to move, her legs now covered in viscous black tar. She tried to pull herself out, but her efforts only caused her to sink deeper.

Probably no more than two or three seconds passed. So why did I feel like I was moving in slow motion as I ran toward the bank? Even Ming and Avery arrived before me. In fact, they were the first ones there. The first ones to reach out their hands. I caught Avery stealing a glance at Rittika as she called, "Hurry! Grab on!"

Thank god, I thought, the world around me turning like a top.

Anne Marie hesitated a beat, then reached for their hands. She had no choice. The tar was already up to her waist. The girls began to haul her up, slowly but surely. And then the unthinkable happened. They let go.

I watched with horror as Anne Marie fell back into that hellhole. In a flash, Pablo and Mel crawled onto their stomachs. They stretched their arms out as far as they could. Their fingers strained to reach Anne Marie, who had gone still, as if she'd given up. Fortunately, Pablo's fingertips managed to catch the edge of her blackened blouse. He pulled inch by inch until he and Mel could safely grab hold of her arms. They quickly hoisted her onto the shore. On dry land, Betty and I tried in vain to pull off the tar that clung to her clothes and body. It stretched like gum, sticking stubbornly to our fingers. The more we tried to get it off, the more of a mess we made. Soon my hands were coated in black.

I kept looking at Anne Marie's face, waiting for her to react. But she didn't. She seemed to be in the same numb state she'd been in after the monkey attack. Only now it was worse, because she didn't even open her eyes. She couldn't. Her lids and lashes were covered in sludge. Betty, Pablo, and I—we talked to her gently. But she made no effort to reply.

Leaving Anne Marie's side, Pablo stalked up to Avery and Ming. He was red-faced and furious. His arms shook at his sides.

"What do you think this is—some kind of sick game?" he cried. Ming looked away. Avery looked at Rittika.

"It's not a game," Rittika piped. She walked calmly over to the trio. "Never has been."

"I don't even know where to start!" Pablo replied, his body shaking, sweat dripping off his skin. "That was the cruelest thing I've ever seen."

"And you say *I* live in an ivory tower," Rittika balked. "This—this cruelty, as you call it? It's how the world is. How it's always been. Some of us make it, and some of us don't."

"And who are you to make those decisions?"

"The way she stepped back—afraid? Ready to give up? I'd say she made the decision all by herself."

I watched Pablo's hands curl into fists at his sides.

"Hey!" Rish called, squeezing between Pablo and his sister. He put his hand on Pablo's chest. "Leave her alone. Ritt didn't push her in."

"She might as well have—the way it went down!"

"No, man, that's not how it was."

Shaking his head angrily, Pablo looked away. I could tell he was trying to calm down. To control himself. But judging from his expression, he couldn't.

"You know, you're as bad as your sister," he said, voice trembling. "Why didn't you stop her? Don't you have a conscience?"

Now Chester inserted himself into the middle, pulling on Rish, who looked ready to swing.

"And you!" said Pablo, lashing out at his old roommate. "You're the biggest disappointment of all."

Chester shrugged uncomfortably. "What do you want from me, dude?"

"I don't know—a *reaction*?"

"I was an innocent bystander."

Pablo shook his head. "There's no such thing, and you know it."

Guiltily, I realized I agreed with Pablo. His comment made me ashamed for being so passive. Ashamed because maybe there was a reason it had taken a few seconds for me to get to Anne Marie, and that reason was cowardice. Looking at the three boys, one by one, I understood something. Chester wasn't who I thought he was. He looked like the kind of hero you read about in fairy tales: big, strapping, and handsome. But in real life, Pablo had more courage in his pinkie than Chester had in his whole body.

Pablo stepped back. He stared at Rittika and Rish, then at Avery and Ming, as if evaluating them for the first time.

"You're savages," he swore. "All of you." Turning on his heels, he stalked into the jungle.

When he'd gone, I immediately looked at Mel, wanting her reaction. Her guidance. "I'll take Anne Marie to the ocean," she said. She put her hand on Anne Marie's sticky arm and helped her up. "We'll be able to scrub the tar off with water and sand."

"Wait for me," I replied, relieved that Mel was taking charge. Quickly, I stole a last look at the pit, which was once again placid after all that action. I stared at the shiny, reflective layer of water that hid the void below. It was like peering into a dark mirror.

A full hour later, Mel and I had managed to scrape off most of the tar—and unfortunately, some of Anne Marie's skin, too. In all that time, I wanted her to cry, complain, react in some way. Any way. But she remained eerily silent, cocooned deep inside of herself.

Later, the three of us trudged back to Camp Summerbliss in silence. When we arrived, we found a flock of black birds helping themselves to the remainder of an earlier meal on the rock table. Mel charged at them, whipping her knife from side to side. Like a single amorphous animal, they flew into the air—a loud, shifting inkblot against the twilight. One more shadow before nightfall.

———

In the morning, Pablo still wasn't back. He didn't come back the day after, either. Or the day after that. I worried about him constantly, as much as I worried about Anne Marie, who now spent all her time at the lookout or in the jungle. I wondered if he was brooding somewhere, too disgusted by our behavior to ever rejoin us. I wondered if he'd fallen into a trapping pit or gotten into an accident. My worst fear was that the enemy had found him, alone and vulnerable.

With Pablo gone, we seemed to lose faith in ourselves, and our plan to get off the island lost momentum. At the same time, the organization we'd established in the first days began to erode. For some, it was just an hour. For others, it was three, or five, or a whole day. People were skipping their chores to sunbathe, swim, or nap in the damp of the jungle. The campfire was going out frequently; everyone assumed someone else would relight it. Ming told us to cook our own breakfast; she wanted to sleep in. At night, only Mel, Betty, and I patrolled.

Believe it or not, even Mel was beginning to slack. She spent long hours looking for ibises. I couldn't tell one bird apart from the next, but she had identified six distinct individuals. In her notebook she sketched them and gave them names. She wrote about their locations and behaviors, habits and diets. Her fixation was so consuming that I sometimes had to remind her to come back to camp.

After the tar incident, I stopped wanting to have anything to do with Rittika. Almost. That was the terrible thing. Even though I hated what she'd done, and wanted to hate her, period, I didn't. I couldn't. She still captivated me. It was hard to come to terms with how someone so beautiful could also be so ugly.

Against my better judgment, I still hung out with her. I still clung to the compliments and offers she tossed to me like candy.

"When we get back home," she said one afternoon, "we should vacation together, you and me. You can come to our house in Switzerland. You'd love it. It's beautiful. And Swiss boys—they love brown girls. Sorry, *gold* girls."

I blushed.

"So you'll come? To Switzerland?" she asked. "Or Buenos Aires, maybe. We've got a place there, too, right on the beach. It's sick. The clubs, the shopping, the surfers, the restaurants. Everything is *amazing*."

I nodded, trying to solve a question in my mind, whether I'd rather tromp through the backwoods of Maine with the Sharpe sisters or go clubbing in Argentina with Rittika. I couldn't decide.

"So, Sam," she said, "tell me something about you that I don't know."

"You first."

She laughed. "Okay. Anything?"

"Anything."

"Hmmm . . . well, I have nightmares almost every night. Terrible nightmares. Usually, I dream I'm a little girl again, and I'm being chased."

"By who?"

"Oh, by just about every evil creature you can imagine. Monsters, vampires, Gollum, Medusa. Sometimes even by kids at school. I run and run, but they always gain on me. And just when I'm about to get caught, boom, I wake up. For a second or two, I don't know if it's really happening—if I'm really about to die, and I'm terrified. It's always the worst part of my day: the very beginning."

"Whoa," I mumbled, too shocked to form a coherent reply. I couldn't get over the fact that Rittika felt terror every night. Rittika, who seemed so indomitable, so fearless. Nor could I believe that she'd admitted it to me.

"Your turn," she said.

"Oh god, I've got a million issues."

"Yeah, right."

"Really!"

Her tea-green eyes appraised me. "Samantha, you just think you've got a million issues. That's your real issue."

I waved her off.

"So," she continued, "if you don't want to talk about yourself, tell me something about Mel."

I felt more than a twinge of discomfort. I didn't want to be a traitor. "What do you want to know?"

"Something good. Something juicy."

I stared into the jungle, stalling. "There's nothing juicy to tell. What you see is what you get."

"She is pretty bland," Rittika acknowledged condescendingly. "So why do you hang out with her so much?"

How to explain the lure of the youngest Sharpe sister to someone like Rittika, someone preoccupied with boys and fashion and popularity? It was impossible.

"You wouldn't understand."

"Try me."

"I don't know. I guess I find it fascinating how much she knows about nature. Like, who else our age can make canteens out of gourds, or identify a million animal prints, or extract poison from frogs? It's a gift. She's kind of a genius." A half second later I realized my mistake. How dumb could I be? I prayed Rittika wouldn't pick up on it. I prayed that her finely tuned sense of opportunism would malfunction this one time.

"Are you talking about that frog Ming found?"

Oh hell.

"Yeah, but it's nothing."

"Mel found a way to take its poison out?"

"I mean—kind of."

Rittika peered into my eyes. I felt boxed in by her stare. That's the particular power of beautiful people. When you have their attention, they can make you feel exalted and claustrophobic at the same time.

"Yeah, so she caught it. I don't know how, but she did. And then she took out some of its poison—that part was gruesome, actually. She said we should have it," I babbled, "in case we need to use it on the enemy."

The "we," I knew, didn't include Rittika. Not really. But I'd given her an in, and she was way too savvy not to use it.

"So where is it—the poison?"

"I forget . . ."

"Sam . . ."

I knew better, but it didn't matter, not when her eyes were boring into mine. Pretty soon I'd spilled the rest of the secret: where the syringes were hidden in the storage tent.

"Well, that was smart of her," Rittika said, tossing her hair. "Getting the poison and all." She put her arm around me and gave me a squeeze. Enveloped in the clean, sweet scent of her hair, I felt sick to my stomach. "Hey, you want to know something?" she continued. "My dad is a fan. He always says, 'Why don't you invite that nice Indian girl from school anywhere?' I swear he wants you to be my bestie."

Still reeling from my own stupidity, I gave her a skeptical look.

"You don't believe me?"

"I barely know your father."

"But you made an impression."

Maybe I had, I thought, but I doubted it had been a good one. My one and only conversation with Mr. Singh had happened at Drake Rosemont's ninth-grade holiday party. It was a big, splashy affair: punch in a crystal bowl, delicacies folded in paper-thin phyllo dough, a string orchestra with a harpist. A Christmas tree festooned in white lights and Swarovski crystals dominated the center of Drake Rosemont's main reception hall. There was also a menorah, a basket of dreidels, and a Kwanzaa kinara. I assumed Mrs. Duval, ever obsessed with diversity, had insisted on those.

Most of the school's ninth graders and their parents had been in attendance. The boys looked like they'd borrowed their fathers' tuxedos. The girls *had* borrowed their mothers' jewelry. I hadn't borrowed my mother's—which was costume, anyhow—but I was wearing one of Betty's dresses. My breasts barely filled out the top, but it didn't matter. It was an expensive LBD with a matching velvet stole, and I felt good in it: sophisticated, elegant, and grown up.

Parents talked with one another as we kids loitered in clusters. The musicians played upbeat holiday fare: "Jingle Bells" and "Joy to the World." You could tell my classmates and I wanted to dance by the way we bobbed our heads and tapped our feet, but we didn't, because looking cool was more important.

I had known Mr. Singh was there. Everyone knew. When he made an appearance at a school event, it was like having a celebrity in the house. Even at a wealthy, one-percent place like Drake Rosemont, Mr. Singh stood out. There was something mysterious and decadent about him, and it wasn't hard to figure out what it was.

"Yeah, the billionaire," I heard a curly-haired girl whisper, pointing. "My dad read about him in *Forbes*."

When I found myself next to him at the punch bowl, I felt starstruck. He smiled and said hello. I almost had to pinch myself.

"Another beautiful Indian girl, like my daughter," he said. "Do you know my Rittika?"

I smiled back. Mr. Singh was neither tall nor distinguished-looking, but his eyes were as pale green and nimble as Rittika's. I blushed when I looked into them.

"Yes, sir."

I hoped the conversation would be short. By ninth grade, I'd already taught myself a protocol around Indian people. Smile, listen, don't talk too much.

"Are you having a good time?"

I nodded, worried that the unraveling of my Indianness was about to begin. If Mr. Singh heard my lack of accent, he'd ask if I'd been born here, in the US. I'd have to admit, yes. Where in India were my parents from, he'd want to know. I'd concede that my father was from Bihar, known for thugs, bandits, and poor people. And my mother? She'd been born here, in America, in Detroit.

Mr. Singh would see then that I wasn't a "beautiful Indian girl" but a diluted impostor. A mixie, as Pablo liked to say. He'd look closer and notice: My hair had glints of blond in it, my skin was too pale—northern Indians tended to be darker. And what of the freckles on my nose and cheeks? Very unusual. Very Anglo.

Did I at least visit India?

No, I'd be forced to say. I'd never been there.

"What is your name, dear?" he asked me, filling my glass with ruby-red punch. I tried to keep my hand from trembling.

"Sam Mishra."

"Ah, 'Sam' for Sampatti?"

I shook my head.

"Yes, I know, Samiksha."

"No."

"Samaah?"

"No—it's Samantha."

"Your parents named you Samantha . . . Mishra?"

"Yes."

He was silent, lost in thought.

"Samantha, have you ever been to India?"

Here we go, I thought.

"No, sir."

"Why not?"

There were numerous reasons. My mother didn't want to go. My sister's health was never good enough. Such a trip would be too expensive. And the main reason: My father's relatives had disowned him when he'd abandoned an engagement back home to marry my mother.

"It just hasn't worked out yet."

"It will work out. One day."

"I hope so."

"Don't have hope. Have certainty."

Conversation ceased then. Mr. Singh continued to look at me, but now it was a different look, infused with what seemed like pity.

"Nice to meet you," I told him, my punch glass filled too high, so that it sloshed in my shaking hand. Liquid dribbled onto my dress. I wondered whether dry cleaning would be able to remove the stain or if I'd owe Betty. There was no question the dress cost way more than I could afford.

"Nice to meet you, Samantha," Mr. Singh replied.

I tried to catch his eye one last time, but he was already looking at something or someone else. I deposited my cup next to the punch bowl and practically ran away, feeling overcome with shame, pride, or both.

TWELVE

I MADE IT A POINT TO CHECK ON ANNE MARIE AT least once a day. She was barely at camp anymore. She returned only as night crept in, and kept to herself, alone in her new tent. I knew she was slipping away, the same way I'd seen my sister, Alexa, slip away, but I was determined to help her as best I could. Armed with food, I made the long walk through the jungle to the outcrop at the edge of the island. Usually, I found her sitting cross-legged on the lookout, perfectly motionless, gazing at the ocean.

But one day she wasn't there. Instead, I found a tall column of round stones. The stones were balanced precariously, one on top of the other. I knew they wouldn't stay there for long. One strong gust of wind and that teetering column would collapse, stones rolling like balls every which way, even over the precipice.

I wasn't sure why Anne Marie had made that column— maybe for no reason at all. But it troubled me. With a sword in my hand, I wandered the jungle, calling her name. I tried not to think about the enemy, boars, or pits. I did think about Pablo, though. I hoped I would spot him. I wanted to tell him that I missed him. I wanted to ask him to come back to camp. But like so much else on this island, he'd become elusive.

Eventually, I began searching the area of the giant trees. This part of the island remained one of my favorite spots. The otherworldly size of the trees never ceased to amaze me. Tired, I took a rest and a long drink from my gourd canteen. Then to my surprise I spotted Anne Marie. She was leaning against one of the huge roots that slithered along the ground. Overhead, the tree it anchored seemed as tall as the mountain on the north side of the island.

"I've been looking for you everywhere," I called out. When I reached her, I tried to give her a hug, but she pulled back.

"Shhh! He could be listening," she whispered.

"Who?"

She looked over her shoulder. "The beast."

"Do you mean the enemy?"

"I've seen him here before."

"You have? When? Why didn't you tell us?"

She didn't answer but instead began to climb the tree whose root she'd been leaning on. She had no trouble scaling the trunk, using vines and deep impressions in the bark as hand- and foot-holds. It was clear she had done it before, perhaps many times. I hesitated, then attempted to follow her, fumbling, scrambling, scratching myself. From below I marveled at how skinny her bare legs were. Skin and bones covered in mosquito bites. I doubted she weighed ninety pounds.

About fifteen feet up, she pulled herself onto a branch that ran nearly parallel with the forest floor. It was as wide as a park bench. With great effort I managed to join her. I had to catch my breath. My hands, feet, shins, and knees were so scraped they tingled.

"Nice view, huh?" she said.

I surveyed the jungle. The other giant trees blocked some of the view, but still it was fascinating to see the island from the level of the canopy. Everything seemed a little smaller, a little more manageable.

"Do you come up here a lot?" I asked.

"Yeah, I've got a spot. A special spot."

"Right here?"

"I'll show you."

Nimbly, she scampered away from the trunk along the branch, stopping before a large cluster of leaves. I followed gingerly on my hands and knees. When she halted, I realized that the cluster was actually something else—a nest. Though covered in leaves, it had been constructed with many things: branches, vines, stalks, grasses, moss, even seaweed. These were braided together intricately—frankly, beautifully. There were even some feathers stuck here and there. Looking closer, I realized they might have been ibis feathers. My stomach felt suddenly sick.

The nest was large, big enough for a small person. Big enough for Anne Marie.

"You made this?" I asked.

"Yes."

"Is it, like, an art project?"

"It's a nest."

"I can see that."

I looked at her blankly. Thankfully, she elaborated. "At school I have my dorm room and the art studio. Here I don't have anything, so I decided to make my own place. What do you think?"

Weird. Bizarre. Off-the-wall crazy. "It's . . . impressive."

As she hopped from the branch into the nest, I noticed that her toenails were long, ragged, and unkempt. She sat down, cross-legged, in the middle.

"Anne Marie, what do you do here?"

"I relax, close my eyes. Bide my time, I guess."

"Bide your time until what?"

"Until I figure out how to get home. I never thought I'd miss Drake Rosemont, but I do. I miss it a lot."

"I really think you should stay with us at camp."

"No offense, but I hate Camp Summerbliss."

"Why?"

"You know why?"

"Is it Rittika?"

"It's the beast."

"He's at camp?"

"He's everywhere."

At that moment, I was more afraid of Anne Marie than of the enemy. More afraid of what Anne Marie could do to herself. Clearly, she was losing her grip on reality. I couldn't bring back her medication, but I was sure that being with other people was better than being isolated like this.

"Come on," I urged. "Come back to camp for a little while. We'll go swimming in Conch Lake."

"I can't. I'm working on a project."

"Your nest?"

"No, something else."

"Come on, Anne Marie. I miss you. Everybody misses you. Besides, you could use a good meal."

"I can't," she repeated. "I have to make sure I can get away from the beast." She clenched my arm. Her ragged nails scraped my skin. "You need to get away, too. He's coming—and he's not gonna stop this time."

I felt a shiver run down my spine, but I ignored it. I told myself that she was crazy and that everything out of her mouth was crazy, too. She was roosting in a nest, for god's sake.

I took a deep breath and willed myself not to raise my voice. "Anne Marie, I'm going back to camp and I want you to come with me. If we work together—all of us—I'm sure we can find a way off this island."

Maybe I wasn't convincing. Or maybe Anne Marie wasn't capable of listening anymore. She began staring off into the distance, leaving me to study her profile: the bony jut of her chin, the protruding cheekbones. I noticed that her ear was full of goopy orange wax. It plugged the entire cavity. A healthier person would have been aware of the problem.

I pleaded several more times, but she tuned me out. Finally, I climbed down the trunk alone, sliding half the way. The rough bark scoured my skin like sandpaper. Biting my lip to keep from crying, I thought about not just Anne Marie but also Alexa. More and more, the two were blending in my mind. Two girls, wispy as ghosts. Two girls who could no longer help themselves.

Twice more that day, I revisited Anne Marie's tree, to make sure she was still there. She was. She waved at me when I called to her from below. Her ability to stay in one spot for so many hours, motionless, struck me as both stunning and frightening.

When I got back to Camp Summerbliss, I found Mel and told her about Anne Marie.

"We have to get off this island," I said.

"Tell me about it," she replied. "The enemy hasn't come for a while. He's due."

It took us a while to gather everyone. Our classmates were scattered all over the island—swimming, fishing, sleeping, gathering fruit. Doing just about anything but taking care of camp or one another.

Mel called a meeting. Rittika and Rish chose not to join, but everyone else did. The cubic-foot exercise had ignited in many of us a feeling of hope. Though Pablo was gone, I think we continued to cling to this hope. To the possibility that we could save ourselves. At night we brainstormed around the campfire, our faces hot as we leaned close to the flames. We needed a method of transport, something that could take us far away from the dangers of the island. Mel told us to put all our ideas out there. Nothing was off-limits.

"Think of the resources here," she said, "and be creative."

Though we talked for a couple of hours, Betty, we all agreed, had the most sensible plan: building a raft out of bamboo canes, which were light and hollow, but also strong. Mel took a vote. Unanimously, we agreed to give it the green light. She urged us to start building the very next morning.

"So that's it? Our solution?" Chester asked her.

"Well, we'll work on one other project, too."

I wasn't sure which one she meant, since the other ideas had ranged from impractical, to silly, to downright ridiculous.

"Which one?" asked Chester.

"My idea—the hot-air balloon," she finished.

A murmur went through the group. Avery and Ming giggled.

"You're kidding, right?" Avery asked, echoing the voice in my own head.

"Not at all," she replied. "The parachute is made of nylon. It used to be called the miracle fiber. It's versatile and hardy—perfect for a balloon."

I admired her confidence, but this time it seemed out of place.

"You're going to take apart the parachute and make it into a hot-air balloon?" Avery asked incredulously.

Mel nodded.

"How will you sew it?" Ming said. "How will you get the hot air inside? How will you get the balloon down once it's up?"

"I still have some details to work out," Mel admitted, putting up her hand to silence the naysayers.

That was the thing about Mel: She had the courage of her convictions. Once she had her heart set on something, she wouldn't give it up. The more the others pressed her, the more obstinate she became. Come hell or high water, she was going to make that hot-air balloon.

The question was why?

I waited until later to speak with her. I didn't want anyone else to hear what I had to say. After Mel and I had finished our shifts, I tried to break it to her gently. "I believe in you—you know I do. But I don't know about this idea. You have to admit, it's kind of . . . out there."

"Rockwell, the pushback I'm getting is exactly what Earhart got when she told everyone she was going to fly around the world."

"And look where that got her. Killed!"

"She was a woman before her time."

"Forget about Amelia Earhart. We're talking about you. You and your idea. And I've got to be honest. This isn't one of your best."

"Does that mean you're not going to help me?" she asked.

I'd rather have been helping Betty on the raft project—call

me crazy, but a raft struck me as less likely to get us killed than a hot-air balloon. But I didn't want to let Mel down.

"Of course I'm going to help you."

During the next few days, everyone began work on the projects. Though Chester initially wanted to help Mel, she convinced him to work with Betty on the raft. Sometimes Ming and Avery helped them, but just as often the girls hung out with Rittika and Rish—doing not much at all.

As for me, I spent that time exclusively with Mel.

The first thing she did was show me some sketches she'd made. According to her drawings, the balloon would be shaped like an inverted teardrop. It would consist of eight long pieces of nylon, wide at the middle, skinny at the top and bottom. These pieces would be sewn together, side by side.

As I studied the sketches, she gave me some background.

"So it's like this," she began. "In the seventeen hundreds, there were these French brothers, the Montgolfier brothers. They figured out if they filled a bag with heat, it would float.

"The brothers kept experimenting. Eventually, they made a huge balloon out of fabric and paper. It was held together by two thousand buttons. When it was filled with hot air, it rose into the sky, just like they imagined. They got more ambitious and added passengers: a chicken, duck, and sheep."

"That sounds like a bad joke."

"It's not."

"So what happened?"

"The balloon flew about a mile from its starting point, then crashed. The chicken broke its leg. The others were okay."

"Is this story meant to reassure me?" I asked dubiously.

"The ride will be dangerous," she admitted. "But no more dangerous than boarding a raft in the middle of the South Pacific."

I nodded, although I wasn't sure I agreed with her.

She filled me in on each step, how we would sew the balloon using the needles and thread from the sewing kit. The hot air would come from burning tar from the tar pit. As for the basket that would carry the passengers—people, in our case—she figured Betty could teach her how to weave one.

"To be honest, my main concern is weight," she said. "To carry just one or two people—plus fuel, water, and provisions—the balloon will need to be, I don't know, twenty thousand cubic feet? That's much bigger than what we're working with."

By the ocean, we spread out the tattered parachute on the sand. We weighted down the edges with stones and got to work cutting and sewing. It wasn't long before I realized how hard the task would be. Despite our lack of knowledge and experience, Mel insisted on expert seamwork: even stitches, no raw edges, perfect knots. The hours were long and tedious. My fingertips tingled, turned numb, then throbbed with blisters.

My eyes, like my fingers, grew exhausted by the strain. Sometimes they ached so much I closed them and sewed blindly. The resulting stitches were invariably crooked. Mel would tut-tut, make me rip them out and start all over. Other times I got in a zone and sewed for a long time in a state of near-perfect concentration. It was liberating to be so completely immersed in something that I lost myself to it. Sometimes while writing, I got in the same zone, able to churn out page after page, almost automatically. But most of the time, in writing and in sewing, every minute was a labor. With the balloon, I was painfully aware of each stitch I made, and how many more were needed given the yards of nylon spread out before us.

Even though we caked our bodies with mud, the sun was a problem. The red skin on Mel's ears and the back of her neck began to crack. My skin was as dark as it had ever been.

Grateful for any reprieve from the heat, Mel and I welcomed the rain. As always, the storms came suddenly and torrentially, and the cloud cover that accompanied them felt like a small miracle. So did the cold droplets on our skin.

Once, through the drizzle, I thought I spotted Pablo. I even called out his name. I still thought about him constantly—what he might be thinking or doing. But then I blinked and he—or whoever it was—was gone.

As we got closer to finishing our sewing, I started to come around to the possibility that Mel's whacky scheme just might work. The nylon had undergone a dramatic transformation. Cut, sewn, and repurposed, the fabric didn't look so sad and pathetic anymore. In fact, its new shape held promise. But of the eight pieces of nylon we'd cut, two still needed to be added—and we were running out of thread.

"We can always unravel our clothes," Mel reasoned. "Steal

whatever thread we can from here or there. Or maybe some kind of plant fiber would work."

Fortunately, we finished the whole balloon without resorting to drastic measures. We even had a bit of thread to spare. I felt hopeful when we spread out the nylon once again. Admiring its new shape and form on the beach, I glanced at Mel. I expected her to be just as pleased, but she frowned.

"It's way smaller than I thought it'd be," she said. A light wind rustled the crinkled fabric. "I don't know if it shrank as we stitched it, or if I misjudged the size from the beginning."

The parachute looked fine to me—and quite large, there on the sand. But I couldn't intuitively gauge things the way Mel could. All I could see, as I stared at it, was the hard work and hours we'd put into it.

"Maybe it'll be all right once it's inflated," I said.

"No, it won't. I can tell. It's too small."

"It's only for one or two people anyway. You said so yourself."

During our hours of sewing, I'd tried to picture who would be on board, waving hopefully from the basket as the contraption rose up in the air. I'd also tried to picture who would be left behind, watching from the island as the balloon ascended. In my mind I imagined different combinations of people, but mostly I imagined Mel and me up high, and everybody else below, a huddled mass shouting desperate good-byes.

"The balloon is for us, Rockwell," Mel said, as if reading my mind.

"So we'd just leave the others?"

"We wouldn't *leave* them. With celestial navigation, I know I could get back here. We'd bring help."

"I don't know . . ."

"I do," she replied firmly. "That would be the most logical thing to do. But there's no use thinking about it now. We still have plenty more work to do."

———

Mel collected scrap metal from the plane wreck and began to construct a large, rudimentary trough. It was so heavy we could barely lift it. We ended up dragging it across the jungle to the edge of the tar pit. Mel ladled tar into it with halved coconut shells. Then she set the tar on fire. A terrible smoke filled the air—much worse than the odor of sulfur. Just breathing it made me sick to my stomach.

"I feel like I just smoked a thousand cigarettes," I said, though I'd never smoked even one. I took a long drink of water from a gourd, but that didn't help.

Mel ignored me, too distracted by the goopy, molten-hot tar seeping out of the seams of the trough. "I have to seal these somehow," she said. "The tar's leaking out so fast, there'll be nothing left soon. Besides, any leak would burn right through the bottom of the basket."

I had no answers, and so said nothing.

"Why don't you go ask Betty to help you with the basket?"

she said with a deep sigh. "Or you help them with the raft. I'll figure this out."

I did as told, but first went to check on Anne Marie. These last few days, I'd barely seen her. All I'd done was work with Mel, then return—exhausted and light-headed—to Camp Summerbliss to sleep.

In search of her I traveled first to the giant trees. I found the nest and called her name, but she wasn't there. I decided to walk to the far side of the island, to the lookout. No luck. I didn't see her or the column of stones. There were only a few left on the flat rock where Anne Marie liked to sit. The rest, I guessed, had toppled into the ocean.

I assumed she was somewhere in the jungle, or maybe at Camp Summerbliss. But I didn't want to waste any more time looking. There was too much to be done. Crossing the island again, I joined Betty on a band of beach. She was working alongside Chester. Together, they gave me a progress report.

Motioning to a large pile of wood atop the white sand, Betty explained how they had been selecting sticks, branches, and bamboo canes. Unfortunately, the pickings in the jungle were slim.

"Mostly, we need long, thick pieces of bamboo. But a lot of what we found is rotted," she complained, "or bug-infested."

"And we can't saw fresh bamboo—it's too hard," Chester said. "So we have to use what's on the ground."

"Have you tried cutting it with Mel's knife?" I asked.

"It wouldn't work," Betty replied. "The canes are too tough."

"Dude, I wish we had an ax," Chester added.

"Or a chain saw!"

"You'll find a way," I assured them.

Scattered on the beach were also small rafts in various stages of completion. All had proven defective in one way or another, Betty explained. This one too heavy, that one too leaky.

"We're still experimenting." She sighed. "Do you want to see the one we're working on now?"

She led me to a rectangle on the sand made of four long bamboo canes. Two were roughly fifteen feet long and the other two were roughly ten. Betty showed me her construction technique: laying more canes within the rectangle, side by side, and moving them around like jigsaw pieces. When the canes were tightly fitted, Betty lashed them together with rope she'd made out of braided vines. As always, I was impressed by her skill.

"One of the things we've learned," she said, "is that we'll need pontoons for the bottom—to stabilize the raft and give it lift. Otherwise, it's easy to overturn."

"But we haven't figured out how to make them—the pontoons," Chester added.

"Another issue," Betty continued, "is size. We're not going to be able to make a raft big enough for everybody—not with what's available."

"How many people will you be able to fit?"

"I don't know—four or five? Six at the most." She sighed and rolled one of the bamboo canes with her foot. "I don't want to reenact *Titanic*."

"How's the hot-air balloon coming along?" Chester asked.

"It's got the same problem as the raft," I replied. "Not big enough."

"How many people are we talking?"

I flashed two fingers, like a peace sign.

Chester whistled. "Is Mel worried?" Betty asked.

"A little."

"I could try to help her," Chester said.

"I think she needs some time alone—to think things through."

Suddenly, a monkey came out of the jungle and skulked around Betty's shoes, which she'd left on the sand. When it noticed us staring, it hissed.

"I'm not positive, but I think that's the same one that followed me, Rish, and Pablo on the day of the plane crash," Chester said.

"He doesn't seem very friendly anymore," I replied.

"True. I used to think he was kinda cute, but now he freaks me out."

"Does he come here a lot?"

"All the time."

The creature and I locked eyes for a few seconds. I remembered all too well the way the monkeys had attacked Anne Marie in her tent. I knew I'd never trust one again.

With one more hiss, the monkey disappeared back into the jungle. I shifted uncomfortably and noticed Betty doing the same. Even though we'd been busy with our escape plans, none of us had let our guard down completely. Nor had we forgotten, even for a second, the reason we needed to get off the island. As Mel had said, the enemy was due for another appearance.

"I know you and Chester have your hands full," I said to Betty, "but Mel and I don't know how to make the basket—for the balloon. Can you help?"

She gazed with concern at the jumble of canes and raft prototypes strewn on the beach. Then, with her typical can-do spirit, she smiled and shrugged. "Sure, why not."

THIRTEEN

THE CHANGE STARTED AROUND THE TIME RITTIKA found a dead shark washed up on the beach. It was a little shark, no more than two feet long. It looked more pitiful than menacing, stinking there on the sand, its body rancid, a crab scuttling out of its empty eye socket. Rittika borrowed Mel's switchblade to cut out the teeth. With these she made herself a jagged necklace. The rough triangles, black and gray, wreathed her slim neck and cast a pall over her beauty.

Around this same time, I got my period. I felt nauseated, listless, and mortified. I spent a long time squatting in the jungle and stuffing leaves into my underwear. When I complained to Mel about the cramps, she didn't have much sympathy.

"I'm on the rag, too, Rockwell. Probably most of the girls are. It's because we've been around each other so much. Our cycles are starting to line up." An agitated expression appeared on her face. "Those idiots better not turn Conch Lake pink."

"Gross, Mel!"

But the image stayed with me: Conch Lake sloshing and roiling with blood. It filled me with the same uneasiness as the razor-sharp teeth around Rittika's neck. The feeling persisted when Mel said it was time to inflate the hot-air balloon. Betty and I had woven a huge basket and reinforced it with bamboo to make it sturdy and strong. We'd been optimistic it would do the job. But now that it was showtime, I had my doubts.

Everyone except Anne Marie came to help blow up the balloon. Maybe Rittika had come to mock Mel's efforts, but at least she was there. As for me, I couldn't hide my anxiety. I kept pacing and fidgeting, like I'd had too much caffeine. I scanned the faces of my classmates to see if anyone else was concerned. They didn't appear to be. In fact, most looked excited and impressed when Mel showed them all the stitching we'd done. I even caught a glimmer of hope in their eyes.

Mel explained that the basket would hold only two people. She told them that those two people would get help once they landed. To my surprise, no one complained. I guess my classmates still had faith in Mel. Faith in her ability to get things done, even impossible things. At Drake Rosemont, all the awards, prizes, and honors she'd been given had rankled. Her permanent position atop the class rankings had inspired resentment, especially in Rittika. And her greatest achievement, the Amelia Earhart biography, had sent shock waves through the school, from the headmaster on down. But here on the island, Mel's accomplishments meant something else: proof that she was the leader we needed. The leader who would take us home. All we had to do was trust her.

So why was I so worried?

Mel and I spread the nylon on the beach. She lashed the basket to a palm tree so the balloon wouldn't float away once it was inflated. From our long hours of sewing and talking, I knew that hot-air balloons were normally inflated with industrial fans and burners. We, of course, would be using burning tar. In private, she had admitted the process would be risky. The heat could melt the nylon. Or our skin. There were a million ways for it to go wrong.

Mel positioned us so that we stood in a semicircle. We each held a portion of the nylon over our heads, stretching out the balloon as best we could. Ming and Avery were the ones closest to the hole at the base of the balloon—and to the basket containing the trough. This was no coincidence. There was a very real chance someone would get burned, and though they didn't know it, Avery and Ming seemed to be the sacrificial lambs Mel had chosen.

Stationed between Rish and Chester, I watched breathlessly as Mel lit the tar in the trough. It started to burn instantly. Thick, hazy smoke curled and twisted from the sizzling vat. The smell was wretched, as always. My instinct was to put my hands over my mouth and nose, but I couldn't. None of us could. We continued to hold the nylon over our heads, willing the balloon to inflate as quickly as possible.

Unfortunately, the process was slow. While the fire raged, Avery and Ming held open the mouth of the balloon at an angle, pointed toward the smoke. Meanwhile, Mel fanned hot air into the balloon's opening, using palm fronds.

The minutes ticked by very slowly. My arms grew tired. My lungs felt like they were caked in soot. For a long time I suspected that we were making no progress. The yards of nylon were limp, gravity pulling them toward the ground even as we held them up. Most of the hot air seemed to be going around the hole rather than into it. But eventually, air pockets began to ripple inside the green fabric. Less effort was required to hold up all that nylon; the hot air was taking effect. I stood on my tiptoes, glancing over the edge of the basket to see if there were any leaks in the trough. So far, so good.

"Hands higher!" Mel called.

The balloon's hole trembled like an open mouth. I could see Ming's and Avery's arms trembling, too. Their job was tricky as well as dangerous. Both girls had to be close enough to the smoke and flames to let in the hot air, but not so close that they hurt themselves or damaged the balloon.

"I'm burning up!" Avery complained, not for the first time.

"Hold steady. It'll get better. Once it's more inflated, you can step back."

"I'm burning. Seriously."

"Hold steady," Mel repeated sternly.

"I can't!" Avery snapped. There was genuine anguish in her eyes. Both girls looked downright sick, coughing and lurching, tears streaming down their faces as they repositioned their arms. Meanwhile, Mel waved the palm fronds frantically, like a bad cheerleader. I almost couldn't bear to watch.

I knew there had to be a better way to do the job. Maybe we could make a funnel from the top of the trough to the base of the balloon? Maybe we could make a huge, hollow tube connecting the two? Mel's fanning just wasn't cutting it. She knew it, too. I could tell by her eyes, which were teary from the smoke, but also panicked.

Finally, the small air pockets inside the nylon began to coalesce, forming one giant pocket, which pulled the balloon up and into the sky. Avery and Ming, red-faced and soaked with sweat, at last let go. One by one, the rest of us did, too. The balloon rose dramatically. Ten ropes secured it to the basket, which was still on the ground, weighted down by the burning trough.

With the open mouth now directly above the smoking tar, the balloon inflated to full capacity. It was one of the most exciting things I'd seen on the island. One of the most exciting things I'd seen, period. As the nylon swelled, so, too, did our hope. Our chances of getting home—and escaping the enemy—suddenly seemed pretty good. I could sense a new optimism on the faces of my classmates. We stared above in silence, beguiled by the sight of Mel's latest and perhaps greatest creation.

Soon the whole contraption—basket, connecting ropes, and balloon—was aloft, tethered by only one thing: the rope attached to the palm tree. If that snapped, Mel's brainchild would float away forever. Maybe that was on her mind when she decided to board the basket. A test ride on the balloon hadn't been part of the plan. It was too early for that—and too dangerous. But there she was, demanding a boost from Chester. He lifted her and she scrambled aboard, descending headfirst into the basket and nearly brushing against the side of the trough. The basket began to sway dangerously. Though I couldn't see inside it anymore, I suspected some of the tar had spilled out. She must have come into contact with it, or the vat, for she cried out and took a big, tottering step back.

"Be careful!" I yelled, as baffled as I was frightened. Why had my best friend climbed aboard? Why was she being so reckless?

The basket continued to swing back and forth perilously, straining against its leash. Meanwhile, the trough churned out thick, noxious clouds of smoke, making it difficult to see. Mel, off balance, craned her head in the direction of my voice. She wasn't paying attention when the vat began to slide toward her. It must have burned her legs. Grimacing, she bent backward over the edge of the basket and for a second was suspended there, half in and half out. Then she fell.

She landed hard on the ground, her right arm absorbing both weight and momentum. I winced when I heard an unmistakable sound, the soft, sickening crack of bone. I cringed when I heard her cry out.

Everything happened so fast, I could barely register it. Mel's arm breaking, Chester rushing to her side and dragging her away, Ming doubling over in a hysterical fit, the basket falling to the ground, only to flare up in flames. In seconds, yards and yards of precious nylon melted into olive-green Silly Putty. Everything happened so fast, I couldn't even recognize it for the disaster that it was.

I just stood there, immobile and idiotic, repeating Mel's name. Even when Chester and Betty managed to put out the fire, and we abandoned the damaged balloon to head back to camp, the full impact of the accident didn't hit me. I don't know why—maybe I was in denial. Betty found the first-aid kit and pried it open with Mel's knife, only to see that the bandages and dressings had disintegrated. The scissors were rusty, and we couldn't read the labels on the various bottles and tubes. Betty gave up on the kit and went about weaving a sling.

Chester carried Mel into the tent and laid her down inside. Dazed with pain, she passed out. It was the first time I'd ever seen her sleep during the day. Normally, she was averse to even the shortest of naps. "A waste of time," she'd said. "I'll sleep when I die." Even when she'd had mono last year, she'd stubbornly refused to go to bed before ten o'clock at night. She'd stuck to her normal schedule. But now she slept. She slept so deeply that I checked on her frequently to make sure she wasn't unconscious, or worse. The rest of the gang spoke in hushed tones around camp. They tried to go about their normal business, but couldn't.

As for me, I started to wake up from my stupor. As Mel slumbered, I stewed, turning over the accident in my head. But no matter how many times I rehashed it, still I couldn't quite believe how quickly Mel's project had gone from dream to nightmare.

Mel awoke from her nap with a screech so terrifying and raw I felt her pain. I helped her sit up and sip water from a gourd canteen. Betty and I had applied aloe vera to the burns on her legs, but we hadn't touched her elbow, fearing that she'd wake up. Now it had swollen to twice its normal size. The skin was bright pink and hot to the touch.

"What can I do?" I asked her. "Tell me how I can help."

Gritting her teeth, Mel told me to search the island for specific plants. She said there were all sorts of things growing here that could relieve pain. But the names she spoke—goat weed, thespesia, pennywort, candlenut, sorrel, mile-a-minute, arrowroot—meant nothing to me. The only ones I recognized were wild cabbage and mint. Mel tried to sketch the desired leaves, bark, flowers, and roots with her left hand, but the doodles were so messy I had to go by her descriptions alone. The search took a couple of hours, and the whole time I worried for Mel. My mind raced from one awful hypothetical to the next.

What if her arm never healed?

What if she died?

I returned to the tent with a slew of plants that may or may not have been what Mel wanted. She sorted through them, took a few bits and pieces, and tossed the rest aside. She handed me the sprigs and told me to steep them in hot water. When the tea was brewed inside one of the gourds, she drank it. Then she fell into a deep sleep again, her brow furrowed.

When she awoke a second time, she asked me to apply more aloe to her arm and legs. By then her whole body was flushed and sweating. Although she was doing her best to endure the pain, I would have preferred crying and screaming to the quiet agony in her eyes.

"Crappity crap crap," she whispered. "It's bad, Rockwell. Really bad. I'm done."

"Don't be ridiculous. Do you think Amelia Earhart gave up when she was running out of fuel over the South Pacific?"

Normally, the mention of Earhart would have cheered her up. But not today.

"No doctor, sterilization, antibiotics," she said. "God, I really am done."

"At least you've found religion," I tried to joke, rubbing aloe vera gel between my hands to warm it. I applied the gel as gently as I could to the swollen flesh of her arm. Though I touched her lightly, I could feel why she was in such distress. Just beneath her skin was a jagged spear of bone.

This wasn't just a crack, I realized. It was a break, clean and final.

"What?" she asked, studying my face.

"Nothing."

"It's broken, right?"

I bit my lip.

"What good am I going to be like this?" she said. "I won't be able to feed myself, or go to the bathroom, never mind get off the island."

"Listen, just concentrate on resting—that's all. You'll get through this. *We'll* get through this."

I wrapped the burns on her legs with wild cabbage leaves and told her I was going to make more tea. I was eager to relieve her pain, but the truth was, I was even more eager to get out of the tent. I needed to be away from her so I could compose myself. The feel of that sharp bone had terrified me.

At the campfire, Betty intercepted me as I tore more vegetation to boil.

"How's she doing?" she asked.

"Not good."

I told her how I'd touched the broken bone. How I was surprised it hadn't punctured her skin already.

"Can a break like that heal on its own?" she asked.

"You mean, like, without a doctor?"

"Yeah."

"I don't know. I think we have to at least set the bone."

"How do we do that?"

I shrugged. "Look, I don't know what I'm talking about. I just remember reading about bone setting once in a novel."

"What did you read?"

"You have to, sort of, manipulate the bone back into place, which is really painful. And then when it's aligned, you have to bind it against something solid, like a stick. Something that will keep it straight."

"You think that's what we have to do?"

"I don't know!" I was on the verge of tears.

When Betty put her hand on my shoulder, the tears spilled.

"Let's wait for now," she said. "No need to rush into anything."

"All right."

I stuffed the shredded vegetation into one of the gourd

canteens. Then I poured in fresh water and let the brew simmer over the campfire. When it was ready, Mel drank the whole thing and asked for more. As daylight faded, I brewed a lot of tea and stored it in multiple gourds.

It was a good thing I did because that evening Mel sobbed for hours. The pain kept her awake. She guzzled all of the tea. It helped a little, but not enough. In desperation, I got out a bottle of whiskey from the supplies tent. By firelight, the amber bottle glowed. I unscrewed the cap, sniffed, and took a swig. Not bad. I doubted it could make her feel any worse.

Crawling into her tent, I handed her the bottle. "Drink," I ordered.

To my surprise, she obliged. Then she wiped her mouth, lay down, and finally slept.

FOURTEEN

THE FOLLOWING DAY, MEL'S ARM STARTED CHANGING. The skin went from bright pink to bluish purple. As fencers, we were used to deep and painful bruises. At Drake Rosemont we'd worn them proudly—they were the badges of an honorable battle. But Mel's bruises were different. Worrisomely dark. Some as black as frostbite.

"Internal bleeding," Mel said. "My arm is killing me, but I actually take that as a good sign. At least I still have feeling. My muscles and nerves weren't severed."

"But the bone is broken."

She nodded grimly. "We have to assume it's going to get infected, too. If I keep drinking the tea, I think I'll be all right. The pennywort will help—it's antibacterial and anti-inflammatory."

I nodded, glad to hear she was thinking more positively.

Attending to Mel soon turned into a full-time job. When I wasn't helping her drink, eat, or pee, or collecting more plants for her tea, I was updating the others on her condition. Her status was simple. She was the same. Her arm remained swollen, discolored, and extremely painful. The whiskey helped to dull the ache, but it wasn't a palliative, only a mask. And anyway, there were only three bottles of booze. She couldn't numb herself forever. It soon became clear something had to be done. Something drastic.

Betty took me aside.

"You remember what we talked about? The bone-setting?"

"You can't be serious."

She locked eyes with me and I saw that she was.

"Like I said before, I read about it in a novel. It was *fiction*."

"Yeah," she replied, "but the rest of us didn't read that novel. So in a way, you're the most qualified for the job."

"That's ridiculous!"

"Can you suggest someone else?"

"What about you?"

She shook his head. "I can do a lot of things, but I can't do that."

"Why not?"

She shrugged sheepishly. "I'm not tough enough. I faint just getting the flu shot."

I sighed. "What about Chester?"

"He *could* do it. But would you really want him to? Mel's your best friend."

I looked at her face, so plaintive and sincere, and felt myself giving in.

"Will you help me?" I asked.

"I'll try. But don't get mad if I pass out."

Later on, I went to broach the idea with Mel. I brought it up gingerly. To my surprise, she didn't balk.

"I knew it was coming," she said.

"You did?"

"Yeah, if you hadn't brought it up, I was going to."

I felt a rush of relief. "So you know how to set a bone! Of course you do. Why didn't I ask you before?"

"I don't know how to set a bone, Rockwell."

I stared at her, and just as quickly as it had come, my relief faded.

"You must," I insisted. "Try to remember what your father might have told you."

"He never said anything."

"Mel . . ."

"I wish I could help, but I can't. And listen—I can't direct you on this, not when it's my bone you're messing with."

"Mel, you've gotta help me."

"Nope. It has to be done. I get that. But I don't want to talk about it. I don't even wanna think about it."

"Don't you have *any* advice?"

"A little."

I was encouraged. "Tell me!"

"Give me whatever whiskey's left—and make sure someone's holding me down."

It wasn't what I was hoping for, but it was the best I was going to get. After speaking with the others, I decided to attempt the bone-setting that very day, before Mel or I lost our nerve. Betty helped me gather the necessary supplies. When we had everything, Mel lay flat on the ground. Chester knelt over her head, his hands pressed firmly against her shoulders. Avery and Ming each held down a foot. Rish braced Mel's uninjured arm. Rittika watched from the outskirts. And Anne Marie? As usual, she was nowhere to be seen.

I plied Mel with a big slug of alcohol, and snuck a swig myself. It didn't extinguish my worry. But at least my hands stopped shaking.

"Splints?" I asked Betty as I crouched beside Mel's broken arm.

"Check."

"Splint padding?"

"Check."

"Bindings?"

"Check."

"Sling?"

"Check."

"I guess that's everything. You ready, Mel?"

She gritted her teeth and nodded. Delicately, I felt for the severed bones with my fingertips. She let out a gasp.

"Wait a second, doc," Betty said. She ran off and returned a moment later with a small stick, which she placed in Mel's mouth.

"Bite on that," she instructed.

When Mel chomped down, I fingered the two sides of the broken bone, trying to coordinate how they'd fit together again. Mel spat out the stick.

"Don't," she pleaded in agony.

"It has to be done." It was the most firm I'd ever sounded.

She started to squirm, but my classmates kept her still as I applied force to the bones, coaxing them straight. I was surprised by how much strength this required. I used the muscles in my hands, my wrists, even my back to pull and bend her forearm into some semblance of what it had been. It wasn't just the effort that required strength, but the need to counter Mel's resistance. Despite all the hands on her body, she thrashed like a wild animal. Her wailing reached a piercing crescendo. I kept my eyes fixed on her arm, at the job at hand. If I looked at her face, I knew I'd break down.

Thank god Betty remained calm and level-headed. Steadily, she handed me what I needed, item by item. I tried to feed off her energy. When the bones felt aligned again, I pressed padded splints against the inside and outside of Mel's arm. I wrapped the bindings tightly from wrist to elbow and back again. The result was secure and poker straight. Her arm looked like a mummy's.

I wasn't sure if I'd done it right, but I'd done it.

"Finished?" Betty asked.

"Finished."

Ever so carefully, Rish and Chester sat Mel up while Betty helped her put on the sling.

Sweaty, my own muscles strained, I finally looked Mel in the eye. "I did my best."

Her face was wet from sweat and tears. I expected her to yell at me, or ignore me altogether, but she didn't.

"Thanks, Rockwell. I'm proud of you."

It was a moment I was sure I'd never forget, but something tainted it: the sight of Rittika. Out of the corner of my eye, I watched her watch Mel. Her expression was not relieved and thankful, but sly and hungry. The look of a cat who had just cornered a mouse.

———————————

After the procedure, Mel took another sip of whiskey, went back to the tent, and collapsed. I crawled in, too, and lay next to her. More than anything, I wanted to sleep, but I was too wired. I didn't know when I'd come down from the high of the procedure. Resting there beside my friend, I found myself wondering how we'd gotten into this mess. How it had all started in the first place. The journey for me, I realized, had begun years before the crash. It had started when I couldn't stand being home any longer, and taken matters into my own hands.

Alexa had been a junior in high school then. While I still collected stuffed animals and read old copies of *Ranger Rick* and *Highlights*, she talked about boys with her friends and knew how to draw perfect cat eyes with black eyeliner. She wasn't dressing in all black yet, but she had already headed partway into darkness. She was mopey and ill-tempered much of the time. She barely spoke to my parents and was outwardly hostile when my dad told her to study harder for the SATs or to add another AP class to her schedule. He wanted Alexa to apply to Yale but was openly skeptical about her chances.

"If only you were better at maths."

"Math," she snapped. "Singular."

"If you spent half as much time studying as you do texting, you would be a star pupil."

"Dad, no one uses the word 'pupil' anymore."

"You better watch your mouth."

"I will when you watch *your* mouth!"

My father's eyes burned; I could practically see the fire flaring inside them.

"Do you want to be grounded again?" he demanded.

"Yeah . . . that would be great. That way I can keep track of when you visit your girlfriend."

My father struck her, hard, across the mouth. Her bottom lip split open. For a week, there was a crimson zigzag where her teeth had gnashed against softness. Grounded indefinitely, Alexa sat at her desk, an SAT prep app open on her laptop, but all she did was peer out the window, long after nightfall. She looked and listened for telltale signs: the mechanical rumble of the garage door opening, headlights coming to life. Sometimes she came into my room and shook me awake.

"He's gone," she would mumble, half-asleep herself, dark shadows under her eyes, a combination of smudged eyeliner, fatigue, and stress.

"So what?"

"Maybe for good this time."

"I wish."

"We could change the locks."

"What good would that do?" I asked.

"It would send a message."

"He's always going to find a way back in."

"You're right," she said, giving me a kiss on the forehead. I felt the lumpy, zigzagged scab. "Sometimes I forget you're the younger sister."

I might have been young, but I was used to my father having girlfriends. He'd had them for as long as I could remember. When I was little, I didn't understand that there was anything weird or scandalous about my father squiring an ever-rotating group of young women. Their existence was addressed in vague terms, if it was addressed at all. This one was the daughter of a guy who worked at the same plant as my dad. That one was the friend of a friend. What they all had in common was youth, and a particular kind of dusky beauty that Alexa referred to as "Indianness." The girls might have been, outside of our imaginations, Jewish, Italian, Greek, or Persian, but from a distance, they could all pass for *desi*.

As for my mother, she pretended these girls didn't exist. But I wondered if she secretly compared herself to them. If she did, she probably found herself lacking. Blond and introverted—my mother was the opposite of what Alexa and I imagined to be budding Bollywood starlets.

Yet years before, her non-Indianness had been a source of pride. Once, she'd told me the story of how my father had left a girl in India in order to marry her. My mother had seen the turn of events as fateful and romantic, a young man deciding against an arranged marriage to find true love. But as the years passed, the truth came out. And it wasn't romantic at all. The young Indian girl he'd left behind was reincarnated in my hometown. She appeared again and again, with different faces but the same hair. My mother must have realized that my father hadn't abandoned his Indian bride after all but simply found a steady stream of replacements.

My father's girlfriends weren't much older than Alexa was. She knew this because she followed them sometimes. Once, she drove with a friend to the local ShopSmart and trailed my father and his then-date from behind. The girlfriend pushed a shopping cart in high heels and tight jeans, my dad at her side, pointing and advising. Alexa mimicked her wiggly-jiggly walk in my bedroom. I laughed till my stomach hurt.

"Maybe he knows her from work," I managed to say.

"Whatever. She looked like a whore."

I still slept with my Chewbacca stuffed animal, but I was old enough to know what a whore was, and I couldn't get the dirty sound of the word out of my head once Alexa had said it.

A few days later, I opened the door to the bathroom Alexa and I shared to find her on her knees in front of the toilet, her face moist, her hair disheveled.

"Get out!" she screamed. This wasn't the first time I'd caught her. And I'd seen other things that weren't normal: mashed-up pills, a stash of empty cough syrup bottles, long red scratches on the inside of her arms.

I took her words to heart. I shut the door and got on the Internet to search for boarding schools. I wasn't going to run away from home. Hitchhiking and sleeping under bridges sounded pretty stupid; boarding school was a safer bet. Maybe it would be like Hogwarts.

I'd applied to Drake Rosemont for superficial reasons. I liked the hoity-toity name. I liked that it ran from grades seven to twelve, and that there would be kids of different ages. I liked the buildings on the website, how the library looked like a medieval castle, with turrets, spires, and gargoyles. The pictures reminded me of Yale when Dad had taken Alexa and me on a campus tour. Maybe if I got into Drake Rosemont, he would approve. Maybe he'd be proud. It was an odd thought to have when ultimately all I wanted to do was escape him.

I applied all by myself. Drake Rosemont was at the top of my list, but there were other schools, too. Online, I filled out the applications to the best of my ability. I did it in secret so nobody could tell me not to. For the hell of it, I threw in some short stories and poems. I hoped they would set my applications apart.

I got into three of the schools. When my Drake Rosemont email acceptance came, it was accompanied by a personalized note. *"We love your writing, Samantha. It's unique and inspired."* Turns out that the writing samples qualified me for a scholarship I hadn't even known existed.

To be in the running, I had to visit Drake Rosemont for an interview. I told Alexa I needed her help. She was so impressed with my motivation and resourcefulness, she volunteered to drive. We told our parents we were off to visit colleges and they let us go.

We took to the road in Mom's car, the old Subaru. I didn't mind its dents and dings, its rearview mirror reinforced with duct tape. I didn't mind when Alexa cranked up the volume of her music and pressed the gas pedal way too hard. I felt like we were in a spaceship bound for a faraway planet.

I dangled my arm out the window and looked at the smudged mehndi design on my palm. Alexa had applied it the day before. She'd squirted it out of a carrot-shaped plastic bag like frosting, then rubbed in a mixture of lemon juice and sugar to make it set. I'd left on the mehndi only two hours, though Alexa had told me it needed six. The result was too light, the color of a tea stain, only one shade darker than my normal skin.

It was Alexa who had insisted on the bindi, too. She stuck it low on my forehead, almost between my eyes. Then she pushed a pile of thin silver bracelets up my arm. "Made in India, purchased at Target," she said.

"Why so much Indianness?" I demanded.

"You're in costume," she told me. "For the interview."

"Why can't I just be myself?"

"Because being the daughter of an abusive jerk and a pill-popping housewife is not going to get you in."

I cringed, then said, "But being Indian is?"

"You're not Indian," she chided. "You're *half* Indian. Biracial."

"Why does that matter?"

"It's a hook. Being mixed is what's in. What's dope."

"I'm not sure . . ."

"Oh my god, Sam, will you just listen to me? All you have to do is present yourself as mixed, and you're golden."

"But how do I do that?"

"Easy. Talk about the stuff you like in real life, and then throw in Indian stuff. Just make it up, like how you love Indira Gandhi and how you celebrate Holi. Then talk about being pulled between two cultures, and how you're determined to forge a new path. Colleges love that garbage. I think Drake Rosemont will, too."

"That sounds kind of . . . fake."

"Trust me, it's exactly what they want to hear. But you have to back it up with sound bites."

"Sound bites?"

"Yeah, like how multiracial people need to be acknowledged. How it's good that people can check off more than one race on census forms now. How multiracial people have been invisible for too long. Blah, blah, blah."

"Blah, blah, blah," I repeated.

"They'll buy it. You'll see."

"What if my interviewer is mixed race?"

"Please," she replied, rolling her eyes. "Drake Rosemont sounds like a factory where white bread is baked."

I nodded, then thought better of it, and waggled my head from side to side, like our Indian relatives.

On the drive, Alexa had pulled up her sleeves to show me where she'd cut herself again. She showed me how the razor marks were horizontal, because she didn't want to kill herself. "I just like the feel of pain. Isn't that messed up?"

I assured her that it was. It most definitely was.

"Why do you like it?" I asked squeamishly.

She thought for several moments. "It's like I've grown this hard shell. It's probably because of Dad—you know I need to be tough around him. So I cut myself to break that shell. To feel things."

"I don't understand."

"So . . . if I cut myself, or get high, or don't eat, then I get emotional. But otherwise, I'm kind of numb."

"It hurts to hear you say that."

"I know. But I'm the first pancake, right? Bound to turn out bad."

"You're not bad, Alexa."

"Listen, enough about me. It's *your* interview, and I want you to kill it." She glanced at me and smiled. "If you get into Drake Rosemont, you'll be free."

At that moment, I understood that one day my sister's shell might grow too hard, and if that happened, I might no longer be able to get through to her. Already, she saw herself as broken. Even worse, she was addicted to pain. I think my sister loved the perfection of it. Simple and pure, that kind of hurt, while so much at home was complicated, twisted, and ugly.

We drove like there was no tomorrow, listening to a playlist Alexa had made. All of the songs were depressing, and all of them made her strangely happy. When we arrived on campus, she reoriented my bindi—it had migrated to my eyebrow—and gave me a high five.

"You'll do great," she promised.

At first, I didn't say much. I was too nervous about Alexa's instructions. I didn't know if I could pull off her plan. The interviewer, Mrs. Duval, asked me about my extracurriculars, my favorite classes, my writing samples. I struggled to introduce the topic of being mixed; there never seemed to be a good segue.

"Being Indian, do you relate to any Indian authors?" she asked. "Arundhati Roy, Jhumpa Lahiri, Anita Desai? I myself love reading about India. What a diverse country. So vivid, so vibrant, so *colorful!*"

"I'm not sure I relate to any of them," I told her, seeing an in. "Since I'm mixed-race, I don't totally identify as Indian. I'm different—part of a population that needs to be acknowledged. Did you know mixed people didn't used to be counted on census forms? We were invisible for a long time. I'd like to change that."

Mrs. Duval scrutinized me. I could tell from her expression that she was thinking something, but I didn't know if it was good or bad. "What you say is interesting," she replied finally. "If you are selected to be a student here, perhaps you'll consider starting a club for other mixed-race students? I think Drake Rosemont would benefit from that."

I nodded. "Sure, I'll think about that. And for the record," I added, "sometimes I do like to read Indian writers."

When she smiled broadly, I could tell she'd already made up her mind. Alexa had been right.

"You know," she said, "we have some rather high-profile Indian families affiliated with Drake Rosemont. Have you ever heard of a businessman by the name of H. Vijay Singh?

I shook my head.

"Mr. Singh is very supportive of Drake Rosemont. I think it's fair to say he is one of our most generous donors. His daughter and son are students here. They're your age, I believe."

"I'd love to meet them."

She continued to smile and I saw myself reflected in her eyes. I'd become a symbol of multiracialism, the wave of the future. When Alexa asked me how the interview went, I told her I'd nailed it.

Just for kicks, we stopped at an Indian restaurant on the drive home. We ordered mango lassis. Alexa drank hers and half of mine and for once didn't go to the bathroom afterward. I peeled off the bindi and stuck it on the underside of the table, next to an old wad of chewing gum.

The road trip had been one of the best times I'd ever had with my sister. Later, I would come to see it as a turning point. I was off to Drake Rosemont only a few months later, and she was admitted to the hospital for the first time. Apparently, her shell wasn't hard enough to withstand a razor blade plunged too deep.

At the hospital, I told her I didn't have to go away to school. I could stay home and be with her. But she wagged her finger in the air defiantly, despite the IV line and stitches in her arm. "You have to go," she said. "*I* need you to go."

As it turned out, I had no trouble convincing my parents that I should go away. Their attention was on my older sister; they didn't need another distraction. When I showed my dad the pictures of Drake Rosemont's campus, he liked them. He liked my scholarship even more. There was no way we could have paid for even one semester on our own.

"You're the one I don't need to worry about," he told me as he drove me to campus, suitcases and boxes loaded in the trunk and stacked in the backseat. It was my second trip to Drake Rosemont in the Subaru. My mother had stayed home in an Ambien daze. It was just as well. I went crazy when both of my parents were together in close quarters.

I watched my hand trail out the open window, my palm long ago scrubbed of mehndi. There was no music this time. We were crawling in traffic, nowhere near space.

"You've got it together, Sam," my father continued. "Alexa could learn a thing or two from you."

I thought about how my father had one voice for me and another for my sister. He was always gentler with me. He never had that nasty glint in his eye that he had when Alexa was around. I don't know why Alexa was his only target. Maybe they were too much alike, both stubborn and strong-willed. Or maybe she resembled his forgotten Indian bride in a way that made him resentful. Whatever the reason, I hated my father most when he was kindest to me. Right then in the car, I wished he were dead.

FIFTEEN

"I'M SORRY," I TOLD MEL. I'D BEEN WANTING TO TELL her that since the accident. We were still in the tent. She'd just awoken. I'd been unable to sleep.

"Why?"

"Because it was my fault—what happened to your arm. I distracted you while you were in the basket."

"Don't be ridiculous, Rockwell. You played no role in what happened."

"I played some role."

"Not really. It was my own pride that got me in trouble. I wanted the balloon to work so badly, you know?"

"Why did you climb into the basket anyway?"

"I was worried the rope might snap."

So I'd been right.

"But it was never going to work," she confessed. "The flaws were always there; I just didn't want to see them. All I could think about was escaping into the sky—like Amelia."

"Right, but you didn't end up like her. You're still here."

When she smiled, it was more like a grimace. I could tell she was still in great pain.

"When your arm heals," I said tentatively, "maybe you can help with the raft. Betty and Chester are close to making it work."

She nodded and I felt relieved that she'd finally come around. I had a hunch that she'd always known that a raft was our best—our only—way off.

Seconds later, she went quiet. I assumed she'd fallen asleep again, but then I noticed her whole body beginning to tremble. When I touched her forehead, it was burning up. She began to sweat, too. I knew a fever could mean infection. I kicked myself for not preparing tea right after the procedure, for not being prepared.

There was a little pennywort left, thank god. That day I'd found more of the shiny, round, scalloped leaves in the jungle. I prepared the tea as quickly as I could. Mel drank no less than half a gallon before her fever broke, but it spiked again a few hours later. I realized my friend wasn't out of the woods, not by a long shot.

The next forty-eight hours were touch and go. Betty came frequently to help. I welcomed her reassuring presence. But the rest of my classmates, even Chester, were missing in action. I didn't understand how they could abandon Mel in her time of need. At the same time, a part of me was relieved. I shuddered at the memory of Rittika's expression after the bone-setting. Maybe it was better that the others not see Mel so weak. I didn't want to give them reason to believe we were in need of new leadership.

When Mel had finally stabilized and I ventured out of the

tent, what I heard from my classmates gave me the chills. Everyone seemed to have something bad to say about my best friend. How Mel was a control freak. How she had wasted the nylon on a "vanity project." How she was responsible for giving Avery and Ming third-degree burns.

"Her life is one long power trip," I heard Rittika complain.

I had no doubt that she had started the accusations. I took Rittika aside and tried to reason with her. I knew if I could change her mind, the others would follow suit.

"The hot-air balloon was the only big mistake Mel ever made," I said. "Isn't everyone entitled to one mistake?"

She rolled her eyes. "One mistake—sure. But you're forgetting the other hundred."

"Name three," I dared her.

"Number one, she left the bodies of Warren and Jeremiah out to rot. For someone who's always worried about sanitation, that was pretty stupid—not to mention disrespectful."

"Okay, but . . ."

"Two," she said, cutting me off, "she risked Chester's life making him climb up to get that stupid parachute. Because it was *so* important. And three . . ." She ticked off a third finger, but couldn't come up with another example.

"See? She's done way more good than bad," I argued.

"That's debatable."

"We need to listen to her."

I didn't have the heart to tell Mel what was happening—how Camp Summerbliss was turning against her. But I knew I had to tell her eventually. If I didn't, I feared we'd descend into chaos. As delicately as I could, I explained the situation. To my surprise, she said she'd expected it.

"There's no one to keep us in line. No teachers or parents. We've been devolving since we got here."

"What do you think will happen?"

She shrugged pragmatically. "It'll either get better, or get way worse."

Scared, I tried to do my part in the upkeep of our little society: patrolling, keeping the fire going, diving for conch meat. At low tide each day, I wrote in giant letters on the beach *MAYDAY* and *SOS*. When high tide came to wash those letters away, I tried not to get upset. From time to time I thought about going to look for Anne Marie, but Mel was my priority. If I were being honest, I'd have to admit that I abandoned Anne Marie during that period. We all did.

Pablo was a different story. I continued to wish he'd appear suddenly, as if he'd never left at all. He'd look at me with his dark, sympathetic eyes and I'd tell him all that had happened. He'd help me care for Mel. He'd understand how important it was for her to get better. He'd know, intuitively, that her health mattered to all of us. But he never did arrive during those long, dire days. I felt desperately alone as I tried to keep our sinking ship afloat.

There was only one positive consequence of Mel's accident, and that was the clarity it brought. For the first time since the crash, I was able to pause and really open my eyes. I saw that our behavior had become as bad as the state of our camp. We'd gone from being considerate and collaborative to careless and selfish, all in what felt like the blink of an eye. I didn't know how it had happened. Maybe we'd forgotten the rules of normal society. Maybe we'd finally given ourselves over to the wildness of the island. Or maybe we'd been savage our whole lives, rash and animalistic on the inside, and never known it till now.

I knew Mel was almost better when the bruises were no longer black. The swelling in her arm had gone down, too. Little by little, she was acting more like her old self. Then one day she was full of ideas again, speaking urgently of things we had to get done. Of things *she* had to get done.

"They can wait," I told her. "Give yourself another day to get some strength."

To make her rest, I readily agreed to do everything she asked, which is how I found myself in the middle of the jungle, holding her knife. I was on my way to make another tally on the tree. It was still light out, though barely, and I found the V-shaped trunk without trouble. I touched the score marks, like Braille, that Mel had already carved into the bark. There were many of them now—too many. A shudder ran through me as my fingertips registered each and every one.

I opened Mel's knife and began to whittle. And then I heard it: a cross between a whimper and a cry. It was nothing, just one more instrument in the jungle's wild orchestra. But when I heard it again, the humanness of it caught me off guard.

I knelt down and tried to make myself small. Still clenching the knife, I peered in the direction of the sound. It came again, followed by a muffled moan. Suddenly, I realized what I was hearing.

"Someone's hooking up," I whispered, eyes wide. Curious, I plunged quietly into the jungle, making my way toward the sound. Soon I was close—too close. I stopped abruptly, no longer titillated and entertained. I realized what I was hearing.

The female voice was assured, assertive, vaguely British. Rittika's. And the boy's, of course, was Chester's. I wasn't surprised, but I did feel disappointed. And disturbed. I'd hoped Chester would have known better, but I guess he couldn't see past her looks. Or maybe, her looks were all that mattered.

After a while they started to talk. I craned my head toward their voices, trying to make out what they were saying through the din of the jungle. On the island, dawn and dusk were always the noisiest times.

"You like her. God knows why, but I can see you do," Rittika said.

"I don't like her that way."

"Come on, just admit it," she teased.

"What's there to admit? She's different—that's all. Different from anyone else. Even you have to admit that."

"All I know is that she drives me crazy. And everyone fawns over her, like she's freaking Einstein or something."

"You sound jealous."

"Jealous?! Are you kidding me? The *last* thing I am is jealous."

"Why are we even talking about her? It's not like she's leading us anymore. She might as well have broken her neck instead of her arm."

"I wish she had!"

Maybe I should have confronted Rittika and Chester then and there, but I didn't. For one thing, I didn't quite have the nerve. And for another, I didn't see how it would help. Clearly, Rittika and Chester had already made up their minds about Mel. I doubted anything I could say would make them come around.

I just hoped it wasn't too late to influence the others.

———

The next day, I awoke beside Mel feeling groggy. I felt so groggy, in fact, that I didn't register the dread on Ming's face when she peeked into the tent. But then, I swear, I smelled her fear—acrid and sharp.

"On the beach," she whispered, trembling. "An ibis. Someone cut its head off. There's a note, too. On the sand."

"What does it say?" I asked, shivering.

"'Last warning. Get out.'"

Mel sat up abruptly, more alert than she'd been in days. "Take me to it," she said.

We ran to the beach in one petrified drove, Mel and I at the rear. She was still really weak from the infection and I had to help her along. Ming took us to the dead bird. Its severed head lay several inches from its body. There was blood on the sand. Beside me, Mel looked like she was going to puke.

I looked carefully at the message in the sand. It was in the same place where I usually scrawled *SOS*. I didn't think this was a coincidence. The enemy had probably watched me write the message—once, or many times. Maybe he'd watched Mel, too. Maybe he'd targeted the ibis, knowing how important those birds were to her.

I looked away and gazed at my classmates one by one. I was surprised to see that Anne Marie had joined us. It was like she'd come out of nowhere. For a moment, I confess, I suspected her of the killing. It was hard not to consider her isolation and disturbing behavior, the feathers in her nest, the way her toenails were grown out long and ragged, how she talked about "the beast." But her face was as horrified as everyone else's. When I tried to imagine her cutting the neck of that friendly, trusting bird, I simply couldn't.

"That's a set of footprints over there—isn't it, Rish?" Rittika asked.

Mel looked at where she was pointing. "I think there are two sets," she answered. "Look at the . . ."

"I was asking my brother," Rittika said sharply.

"I was only . . ."

Rittika's lancing green eyes silenced her. "Mel, I've talked with everyone," she said, "and we've decided we've had enough of your opinions. They've gotten us nowhere. We're no better off now than we were when we crashed. In fact, we're worse."

Mel stared at her icily.

"You didn't talk with me," I said suddenly.

"What?" Rittika asked.

"I said 'You didn't talk with me.' You said you talked with everyone. But you never asked me about Mel."

"Fine," Rittika snapped. "I spoke with the *majority*. That's enough."

"It's not. We're not back at home. This isn't a democracy. Never has been."

"What are we, then?" she asked sarcastically.

"We're a team. And we've got to stick with the same leader who's gotten us this far." I turned to look at the others. "I think you've all forgotten how much Mel has done for us. Her ideas have gotten us fresh water. They've built fires. They've kept the enemy away."

"Mel's *ideas*," Rittika spat, "have cost lives, wasted time, and broken her own arm."

To my horror, the others nodded in affirmation. Even Betty.

"You can argue all you want, but we know she's a bad leader," Rittika continued. "She only thinks about herself. It's always Mel first, the rest of us second. And as for her ideas, the only good one she's had was putting mud on her skin. I think you know what I'm getting at, Sam." She paused, then said, "You need to choose which side you're on."

Mine or Mel's. The Golds or the Pales.

"I already know," I replied, meeting her eyes. And for once, I had no trouble making my decision. In fact, I'd never felt so sure about anything in my life. Mel was only just recovering, and now she faced a brand-new setback. She needed me, plain and simple. It wasn't about color anymore, or popularity, or even power. It was about family. Here, on the island, Mel was the only family I had.

"What are we going to do about this?" Betty asked Rittika, gesturing toward the ibis.

"I couldn't care less about a stupid bird," Rittika retorted. "It's the note that matters."

"We could take the raft. It's almost ready . . ."

"Forget about the raft. We need to find the enemy and kill him, once and for all."

"We tried that before," I insisted. "We already searched the island, remember? What makes you think this time will be any different?"

"Because now I'm in charge."

There came a cry, shrill and raw. It took me a moment to realize Anne Marie had made it. But by then, she was already retreating into the lawless tangle of the jungle.

SIXTEEN

MY CLASSMATES RETURNED TO OUR CAMP AND collected every weapon available. Disgustedly, I listened to Rittika bark orders. Then I helped Mel take a seat on a boulder shouldering Conch Lake. We dangled our feet in the water. With her good hand, Mel poked at her sling.

"My arm's itchy as hell," she complained.

"Because it's healing."

"God," she said, rubbing her eyes, trying not to cry. "Maybe Rittika's right. Maybe I have no idea what the hell I'm doing, and never did."

"Come on, Mel. You know exactly what's going on. She's talking trash about you so she can replace you."

She sniffed, then smiled ruefully. "Yeah, yeah. I get that. I mean, it happens all over the animal kingdom: the desire to rule. Remember when we saw those ants at Drake Rosemont? Did you know that every ant colony has exactly one queen? One queen ruling thousands? And she'll sacrifice every last one of them to retain her throne."

"It's a brutal world," I said. "Especially if you're a teen-age girl."

"It sure is, Rockwell."

I wiggled my toes, watching tiny minnows encircle my ankles. "This probably isn't the right time to ask you this," I said.

"The right time to ask me what?"

"Can you stop calling me Rockwell?"

She looked both taken aback and amused. "Why?"

"I kind of hate it."

"Really?"

"Yeah, I hate being compared to Norman Rockwell."

"I thought he was a beloved American figure."

"He is. That's why I hate it."

"I don't understand." Nervously, she swished her feet back and forth in the water. My own feet felt heavy, suddenly. In fact, my whole body did.

"For starters, my family is nothing like the families he painted. We're not your wholesome, all-American, white-picket-fence type."

"Oh, come on, of course you are! I've been to your house. It smells like fresh-baked cookies. Your mother wears a gingham apron. Your father puts his hat on a hat rack. You *have* a hat rack. It's by the front door. I've seen it. You *are* the perfect all-American family."

"Trust me, we're not. All you're seeing is surface. Underneath, there are a ton of problems. Especially with Alexa."

"Well, everyone has problems."

"I'm not talking about small stuff."

"What are you talking about?"

"Self-mutilation. Bulimia. Suicide attempts."

Agape, she stared at me. "Why didn't you ever tell me?"

"Because you always call me Rockwell. It's sweet, in a way. I guess I didn't want to ruin your image of me."

"But suicide attempts . . . really?"

"Yeah. And stays in a psych ward. Which really is like in the movies, by the way. Bolted windows, no sharp edges, padded walls, the whole shebang."

"Wow."

"And that smell of cookies? It's your imagination. My mother only cooks, like, twice a year. Thanksgiving and Christmas. The rest of the time she's a zombie."

"What do you mean?"

"She a user, Mel. Sedatives, mostly. She lives on them."

"I'm so sorry, Sam. I wish you'd told me."

"Yeah, I should have. A long time ago."

"And your father?"

"He's the reason my sister can't deal with life."

Now I was the one fighting back tears. Mel rubbed my shoulder as I took deep breaths and tried to hold it together.

"I never told you, but I once studied Norman Rockwell for a report," I said, sniffing. "His life was totally different from his art. Did you know he was a mess? He had four different wives. Four! And one of them killed herself. He had depression, too. Bad depression. So maybe his perfect paintings were an escape. Or maybe they were a Band-Aid. Either way, even Norman Rockwell wasn't Rockwell, if you know what I mean."

Mel nodded, taking it all in. Together, we gazed at Conch

Lake. I noticed some dragonflies buzzing above the surface. They were beautiful, their sleek bodies slicing through the air, their wings diaphanous.

"Damselflies," Mel said, following my eyes.

"I thought they were dragonflies."

"No, they're in the same family, but different."

"How?"

"Damselflies are thinner, more delicate-looking. Pretty predators, I guess you could say. They're amazing hunters. See the way they're hovering right now? They're waiting to strike. As soon as dinner comes along—a mosquito or even a smaller damselfly—they'll nab it."

My eyes still wet with tears, I watched the insects buzzing just above the water. Their bodies were lovely colors: sky blue, metallic green, amber. It was hard to believe that such gorgeous creatures possessed such savage instincts. That they were waiting for just the right moment to go in for the kill.

Then again, I'd seen it before.

Mel and I didn't join the hunt that day. We didn't see the sense in it. No matter how passionate Rittika was about finding the enemy, we knew he was better at hiding than we were at seeking.

Hours later, our classmates began to return, pair by pair, empty-handed. The enemy had evaded them once again, disappearing down his rabbit hole, leaving no trace. Rish and Chester were the last two people to arrive. They loped slowly toward the campfire, necks bent, shoulders slumped. It was clear something had gone wrong.

"We didn't find the enemy, but we did find Anne Marie," Chester said tremulously. "She's on the other side of the island."

"She's—broken," Rish added in a whisper.

"Is she alive?" Mel asked.

Rish just shook his head.

In a haze I followed the group, picturing Anne Marie in my mind. In a morbid corner of my imagination, I saw her atop the lookout tower, where she'd made the ill-fated column of stones. But when Rish and Chester led us to where she lay, it was on the shore below. Her body rested atop a bed of jagged rocks.

We made our way over to her slowly, wanting to avert our eyes. She was on her side, splayed and bent in ways not even a contortionist could have survived. Seawater soaked her skin. A ribbon of kelp twined around her hair. It would have been easy to focus on her body, for she was wearing nothing, and in her nakedness revealed the small, lean bones of a child. Yet it wasn't her body we stared at, but what was attached to it. A pair of what appeared to be—what had to be—wings.

Even wet, sandy, and fractured, those wings were breathtaking. From tip to tip, each was easily as long as Anne Marie's body. As with the nest, she had used the island's bounty to build them: lush palm fronds, fanned grasses, stalks, leaves, and real feathers. I couldn't tell how the wings were held together, but I could see the apparatus that bonded them to her body: the shell and straps of her old backpack. Anne Marie had not disclosed that she still had it. Then again, she'd never been one to reveal much. I hadn't known, for instance, what she'd been doing all this time in her nest. Not just waiting and watching, as I'd thought, but working diligently on a means of escape.

She'd even told me about her project, but I hadn't paid attention.

Anne Marie's creation was just as inspired, architecturally and artistically, as Mel's hot-air balloon. And, in the end, just as futile. I could imagine all too easily what had happened, how she had perished. She would have stood on the very brink of the outcrop, toes dangling over the edge. Maybe she was already wearing her wings, or maybe she'd waited until that moment to put them on. Slinging them over her back, how had she felt? Strong, tentative, certain? I wondered how hard the wind had blown. I wondered if she'd lost her balance or jumped with courage.

I liked to think Anne Marie had made it for a few seconds. In my mind I saw her aloft. *Gust flying.* That's what Mr. Sharpe called it. Riding the wind, rising on each surge, falling at each lull. What seabirds did.

Mel knelt down and ran her fingers over broken feathers and torn fronds. She wiped a bit of sand from Anne Marie's scratched forehead. Nearby, waves pounded and pulverized the rugged cliffs, churning stone into sand. The water, whitecapped and foaming, was treacherous on this side of the island. The reef didn't extend this far. There was no protection against riptides and whirlpools curling below the surface. Any one of them could have been Anne Marie's undoing. Or maybe the fall itself had been enough.

"Tide's coming in," Mel said.

"Maybe that's okay," I replied. Anne Marie had never liked the island. Would it be so bad if the ocean took her away?

I gazed at the choppy gray breakers and thought about how I could have done more to help her. Reality had been slipping away from her for a long time. I'd seen so many signs, and yet I'd mostly ignored them. I hadn't even informed Mel or anyone else about the nest. Maybe if my classmates had known the full extent of her illness, they could have helped her to heal. Or maybe I could have—if I'd tried harder. So many regrets. But there was nothing to do about them now except turn them over and over in my head.

As my classmates and I stood on the shore, sloshing water crept toward us, inch by inch. Then it began to close in on Anne Marie.

"Leave her be," Rittika said authoritatively. "We need to concentrate on the ones who are still alive."

With a shudder I realized Mel had said the same thing about Jeremiah.

———————————

Later on, thoughts of my sister came to me unbidden. Now that I'd failed to save Anne Marie, I wanted more than anything to be there for Alexa. I promised myself that if I had the chance, I would. If I made it home, I would no longer let my parents, or my own fear, stand in the way of helping her.

The problem was, I didn't know if I'd ever make it home. Maybe Alexa and I would always be separated by whole continents and oceans. Maybe that last road trip in the Subaru was the final adventure we'd ever have together. Maybe I'd never get to tell her how much I loved her.

I was too heartbroken to fight my guilt. Too miserable to do anything but stew in self-loathing. When I saw raw conch meat on the rock table, I swiped it without a second thought. I didn't know whom it belonged to, and I didn't care.

Returning to the jungle, I found a secluded spot. Craning my neck, I tried to get a look at the birthmark on my shoulder. Without a mirror, I couldn't see it well. But I knew it was there. A colorless ghost that followed me everywhere. Alexa had more obvious signs of deficiency: scars, brittle hair, a perpetually sore throat. But I'd never doubted that there was something wrong with me, too. Something inherently and irreversibly flawed.

I took a big, fat, flesh-colored wad of conch meat and shoved it into my mouth. It went down easily enough, and I ate more. Great big bites of it, as much as I could stuff in. I'd never eaten it raw before, but I did then. Raw, briny, chewy, primal. So much I gagged and nearly threw up. But I didn't. Juice running down my chin, I held it down. I held all of it in.

SEVENTEEN

"MEL AND I WANT TO KEEP WORKING ON THE RAFT."
I said. "Will you help us?"

I'd found Betty at the borderland between Camp Summerbliss and the jungle. She tore off the skin of a kiwi, a fruit we had only recently found on the island. She pulled the brown-green pieces off bit by bit, as if the task required utmost concentration. Finally, she shook her head.

"I told Rittika I'd keep hunting the enemy. That's more important than the raft."

"Says who?"

She squinted at me, a furrow appearing between her eyebrows.

"You and Mel can finish the raft by yourselves," she replied. "I don't care."

"But you and Chester know everything there is about it."

"I doubt Chester would be interested either. He got up at dawn to make more spears. He'd rather kill the enemy and be a hero than leave and be a coward."

Suddenly, I felt like I was talking to a brand-new person. "Betty, what are you saying exactly?"

She shrugged.

"Are you saying you want to stay here?"

The crease between her eyebrows deepened, and she stared at me defensively. "I like it here. I feel like I've got a purpose. What's wrong with that?"

"Nothing."

"You're judging me. I can tell."

"It's just—what about your family? What about *home*?"

"I guess this feels like home now."

"Home shouldn't be this dangerous."

"Don't act like you have all the answers, Sam. Don't act like Mel."

I was so frustrated I wanted to scream. I dug my fingernails into my palms. "Betty, it could all fall apart! Think about Anne Marie!"

She shook her head as though I couldn't possibly understand. "Listen. Since we got here, I've climbed mountains. Hunted with spears. Woven fishnets. Held my breath and dived to the bottom of the ocean. At night I sleep in a tent that I made—*all by myself*. I never knew I could do those things. I never knew . . ."

Despite my better judgment, I felt a rush of sympathy. She sounded so self-assured. I didn't know what I could possibly say to convince her that she was wrong. And then there was the little piece of me that wondered if maybe she wasn't wrong. Maybe she really did belong here. Maybe her wanting to stay had less to do with choosing sides than with forging her own path. Maybe I was the one who was being shortsighted. It was an unsettling possibility.

I told Mel about the conversation. She was not nearly as emotional.

"Then it's just us, you and me," she replied stoically.

"What about Pablo?"

"Sam, if Pablo wanted anything to do with us, he would have come back by now."

With a heavy heart, I nodded, knowing she was right. We walked to the beach where Betty and Chester had spent so many days raft building. Their latest and final prototype was a little bigger than the one I'd seen. It was also thicker. Dragging it into the water with Mel, I hoped its extra bulk would make it more buoyant. At first it floated just fine. But when we scrambled on top of it, it sank several inches. Water sloshed over the sides and through the cracks between the canes. Mel frowned. I knew what she was thinking. The sea was calm here, but out on the open water, it wouldn't be nearly as forgiving. If we set out on the raft, here and now, we might as well sign our own death certificates.

"Betty once said we need pontoons. Looks like we still do," I said.

"No kidding."

"Would pontoons keep all this water from coming through?" I pointed to the cracks.

"Not necessarily. But I have a solution for that problem." She squeezed water out of her hair, which had turned white blond from constant sunlight. "Let's drag this monster to shore."

Back on dry land, Mel told me we needed to revisit the tar pit. Honestly, it was the last place I wanted to go. The tar pit was now a bastion of bad memories. I'd never be able to erase the image of Anne Marie being dropped into that sticky black wasteland like a piece of trash.

"I think I'll stay here," I told her, shivering.

"You can't."

"Why not?"

"Because I can't carry the trough with one hand."

I gaped at her. "Seriously?"

The trough was another thing I'd sooner forget.

"Seriously."

"God, I hope whatever plan you have in mind is better than the last one."

She scratched at her healing arm and shot me an amused look. "Could it be worse?"

Slowly, soaking in sweat, we hauled the heavy trough through the jungle to the pit. By the time we arrived, my arms felt leaden from the effort. By the side of the pit, we scooped up tar with halved coconut shells and deposited it into the trough. We filled it a couple of inches, then dragged it all the way back to the beach. There, I collapsed on the sand and drank all the water from my gourd. I was so exhausted I could have gone to sleep, but Mel insisted that I help her make a small fire. We lit it beside the trough, then watched the tar begin to warm. Slowly, it began to simmer and bubble. I stirred the black brew with a bamboo cane while Mel collected handfuls of dry grass.

"We're going to use the tar to caulk the chinks between the canes," she said.

I had suspected as much, but was glad that she'd confirmed her plan.

"Will it work?"

She nodded. "Sure it will. Shipbuilders have used tar for centuries. If we fill every crack and crevice, we can make the raft airtight."

"Will we still need pontoons?"

"Probably. But at least this will be an improvement."

As Mel explained what we needed to do, I could tell that she'd already thought through the process. She'd probably been thinking about it for days. First, we stuffed the dried grass into the chinks. Then we whittled sticks into thin, flat paddles with her knife. These were our "caulking irons," Mel said. We used them to apply the tar in the stuffed chinks. When we finished that step, we let the tar cool a bit, then patted it flat with the soles of our oxfords.

Our methods weren't very sophisticated, but they seemed to work. Once we got going, we moved swiftly. The slowest part was waiting for the tar to set. Mel said we should give it the night. The cool evening air would do the job, and by morning— if all went according to plan—the tar would be firm, rubbery, and leakproof.

We finished sometime after dark, then trudged back to Camp Summerbliss, feeling satisfied, but dead tired. We didn't have the energy to dive for conch, so we ate a dinner of bananas. After that, I took a quick dip in Conch Lake. Near the outcrop, Rittika, Rish, Avery, Ming, Betty, and Chester were playing chicken, laughing and splashing raucously. Now more than ever, it was clear we were divided.

Mel and I went to bed soon after. I thought I'd fall asleep right away, but I found myself thinking about Alexa again. As if reading my thoughts, Mel told me she couldn't wait to get back to her sisters.

"I feel like I'm missing a part of myself," she whispered. She told me she'd written them notes, put them into capped water bottles, and tossed them into the sea—even though there was virtually no chance Drake, Gaspar, Tasman, or Leif would ever receive them.

"Still," she said with a sigh, "you never know."

Moments later, Mel fell asleep. I could hear the others still talking by the light of the campfire. They seemed to be reconfirming their commitment to finding the enemy. Not surprisingly, Rittika's voice was the most strident. She said they'd look for him again tomorrow. And the day after. And the day after that, if necessary.

"Sooner or later," she said confidently, "he has to come out and play."

The next morning, Mel and I woke up with the rising sun. Mel made another mark on the V-shaped tree and then we headed back to the beach to check on the raft. I touched the tar with my finger and was elated to feel it bounce back from my touch.

We poured seawater onto the black seams and watched it bead up and roll off. Mel gave me a triumphant high five.

"What next?" I asked excitedly. "The pontoons?"

"I still don't know how to make them."

A little of the morning's shine wore off.

"So what do we do now?"

She scratched her head, then smiled broadly. "We make sails."

I couldn't help but smile back. "With the nylon."

"Yeah."

"Let's get to work."

It had already occurred to me that we could make sails from the nylon. I had a hunch it had occurred to Mel, too—and maybe the others. But Mel had been so hell-bent on making her hot-air balloon, no one would have been able to wrangle the nylon from her.

We retrieved the damaged fabric from the supplies tent. Then I helped her spread what was left of it on the sand. It didn't look promising. During the fire, the majority of the nylon had burned up, and what remained was smoke-stained and singed at the edges. But there was enough—just enough. And if I squinted hard, I could see it: two sails—small, but trusty and true. Sails that could catch and harness the wind, and take us all the way back to where we'd come from.

Mel and I drew in the sand with our fingers, imagining the fabric reincarnated: upright and triangular, straightened by a mast, by the tension of rope, reinforced by bamboo canes.

Mel's attempts at a design were messy, and she soon grew

frustrated. Her control of her left hand was getting better, but it was still a work in progress. More and more, I felt like I was her right-hand man. Literally.

After about an hour we arrived at a plan that we both agreed on, then got to work. We labored through the morning and past high noon, the scorching sun blazing down. I'd forgotten how hard and tedious it was to sew the nylon. How holding the needle for hours made my fingers cramp. Despite the discomfort, we had to be even more careful than last time. There was very little thread left, and no room for error.

When we'd finished, we were as spent as we'd been yesterday. Mel said she'd forage for fruit; I volunteered to fetch more fresh water from the outcrop at Conch Lake. We agreed to meet back at the beach in a little while to test the sail, but on my return, I became distracted. I remembered how Mel had said she'd written to her sisters, tossing plastic water bottles back into the ocean. I thought about how those bottles had already traveled hundreds, maybe even thousands of miles to reach our shores, and how they could probably travel many more. Plastic bottles, naturally light and sturdy.

Naturally buoyant.

The full gourds sloshing in my hands, I ran to the supplies tent. My fatigue vanished suddenly, replaced by a swell of adrenaline. Inside the tent, I stared at Rittika's heaping pile of water bottles. There had to be a couple hundred. Enough, I thought to myself.

Before, I'd felt revolted by that gleaming tower of litter. But now I saw the bottles in a new and redeeming light: not as garbage polluting our oceans and killing our planet, but as an unusual way to stabilize the raft.

I grabbed one of the bottles, the gourds now forgotten, and dashed all the way to the beach, back to Mel. Catching my breath, I excitedly explained my idea.

"Crappity crap crap. That's brilliant!" she said when I'd finished.

With new momentum, we talked about how to make the pontoons. The best idea, we decided, would be to stuff the water bottles into large, missile-shaped mesh bags woven from vines.

"I've watched Betty," I said gamely. "I think we can do this."

After another high five, Mel set out to find long, slim, sturdy vines. She cut them with her blade and brought them back to the beach, where I tried my best to weave them together.

Hours of trial and error passed. The sun began to descend all too quickly.

"I can finish," I said stubbornly, squinting through the dim light.

Mel saw I wasn't going to stop. Quietly, she set about making another fire so that I could work into the night.

The stars were shining by the time we finally finished. The nets were messy-looking, like quickly-cobbled-together craft projects. But they did their job. They kept the water bottles together. Under the constellations Pegasus and Pisces, Mel and I rolled one of the pontoons across the beach and into the water. It performed as we'd hoped, bobbing like a giant buoy, staying well above the waterline even when we climbed on top of it and rode it like an inflatable pool toy.

We laughed with happiness, than hauled it back onto the sand and stared at it.

"I guess my father was right," Mel said.

"What do you mean?"

"All the tools we need really are right in front of us."

By the time we reached Camp Summerbliss, everyone else was already tucked inside their tents. We didn't sleep very well that night. We were too excited. We were so close to our goal. All we had to do was attach the pontoons to the raft and gather some supplies.

"We'll do a test run tomorrow," Mel said into the darkness.

I knew what she was implying. If the test run went well, we could leave. I'd thought about this moment for so long, yet now that it was almost here, I didn't know what I felt more—relief or anxiety. Anything could happen here on the island, but anything could happen out on the water, too.

The next morning, we didn't talk about what was to come, only about what had to be done in the here and now. We attached the pontoons to the bottom of the raft with homemade rope and more vines. With only one hand, Mel tied knots that would have made her father proud.

Betty had already made rough oars. With these in hand, we climbed aboard the raft and pushed off. As we glided over the shallows, watching bright fish flit through crystal-clear water, I knew the raft was going to work. With the addition of the pontoons, it barely sank an inch. The tar had set nicely, and it was as waterproof as a rain slicker.

I was feeling a hundred percent confident until we reached the underwater marker of the reef. As we crossed that dark threshold, I felt my stomach drop. I tended to see the ocean as bisected: the part inside the reef being safe, the part beyond it, not. I didn't like the look of the outer ocean: its dark color and choppy breakers, the way it seemed to stretch on forever. I was alarmed by the rugged whitecaps and the sharp fins that occasionally sluiced through the surface.

Mel pulled in her oar and adjusted the sails, which rustled and flapped. The wind grew stronger, pulling us away from the island more rapidly than I expected. The raft began to bounce and jostle, holding its own against the current, but making me queasy. I motioned to Mel that we needed to turn back. She nodded and adjusted the sails again. Seconds passed and our raft headed farther out to sea. A horrible thought seized me: What if we couldn't turn the ship around? What if we became stranded out on the water with no water or provisions?

But I shouldn't have doubted my friend. Moments later she got us turned around. Slowly but surely, we began to sail back to the island.

"This baby's unsinkable," she shouted to me gleefully, a spark in her eyes.

"Don't jinx it!" I shouted back, knowing very well that our raft was anything but.

"We could leave today," Mel said breathlessly when we reached the shore. Together, we dragged the raft out of the water.

I felt an electric pulse run up my spine. "Do you want to?"

She nodded. "For our sisters."

We left the raft and oars high on the beach, beyond the tide line. As we began walking back to Camp Summerbliss, I asked a question I wasn't sure I wanted the answer to.

"Mel, what do you think our odds are?"

She rubbed her bad arm. "Do you really want to know?"

I nodded.

"Fifty-fifty, at best. But realistically? A lot lower."

"And if we stay on the island?"

"About the same."

"Are you going to feel bad," I asked. "Leaving everybody?"

"We're not leaving just for ourselves, Sam. We're leaving to get help."

"But they don't want help. They don't want to be rescued. Betty told me that."

"Sure, she says that now. But can you honestly see Rittika here a year from now? Five years from now? She'll be totally unhinged. They all will. Bad things will happen. Very bad things," she finished ominously.

I stared at her, not sure what to believe. Not sure of anything. I knew only that we were about to take the biggest risk of our lives. We were silent for a time, then Mel began to discuss preparation. It was easier to talk about the logistics of leaving—how many water gourds we'd need, how much conch meat, coconuts, and seaweed, what the currents and winds and weather conditions might be like—than to reflect on the right or wrong of it.

"A tarp would be nice. To catch water, if it rains. But we already used up all the nylon."

"We could use our tent as a tarp," I said. "It wouldn't catch water, but at least it would give us shade."

She smiled at me appreciatively. "Not bad, Sam. Not bad at all."

We locked eyes, and I knew she was thinking the same thing I was. There was one question we'd so far avoided. Maybe the hardest question of all. How were we going to tell the others?

Back at camp, I didn't expect to see my classmates. I figured they'd be out in the jungle, continuing their futile search for the enemy, but to my surprise, Rittika and her brother were swimming in Conch Lake.

I went to the shore and rinsed off my hands and face. There,

I watched her lean body zip through the water, her long dark hair trailing after her like a mermaid's. She surfaced, appeared to take a breath, then dove under. She was gone so long I couldn't help but think of our arrival on the island, when she'd dived off the outcrop. Then, we'd all thought she'd drowned. This time, I knew better.

She surfaced eventually and called to Rish. I watched him eel his way to her, his strokes swift and elegant. When he looked at what she was holding, he whistled. Eventually, they swam to shore. We greeted each other perfunctorily, like strangers. I wondered how it had come to this.

What Rittika had found was a conch shell. The biggest yet, almost twice the size of any we'd previously caught. She turned it over, declared it hollow, and then did something none of us had ever done before. She put the spiral tip to her lips and blew. I didn't know what she intended to accomplish. But then I heard the sound: a deep, lonesome boom that seemed to spread out over Conch Lake and through the jungle, ricocheting off the trees and the peaks of the mountain. She blew again. This time a bass note, a plaintive cry at the lowest octave, solemn and penetrating.

Mel came stumbling toward me, as awed as I was by the sound.

"How did you do that?" Rish asked. Rittika looked at him, then at Mel and me.

"I don't know," she replied. "It just came out."

The jungle seemed to go quiet. I wondered if every bird, boar, lizard, and monkey was listening.

Rittika blew the conch again. Chester came running out of the jungle as if lured by the sound. Minutes passed and the others came, too. They gathered around Rittika in a circle, leaving Mel and me beyond the periphery.

Since everyone was together, I resolved to tell them that Mel and I intended to leave. But just as I made that decision, I heard a distressing noise. Avery began to scream, just as she had the night after the crash, when she'd complained of a man touching her in her sleep. To my horror, I saw two more figures crossing the threshold between jungle and camp.

A very old man, hunched and wiry. And someone familiar. I froze, wondering if what I was seeing was real.

"Man, Pablo, is that you?" Chester asked tremulously.

EIGHTEEN

WE COULD ALL SEE THAT IT WAS. IF NOT PABLO, THEN his ghost. He was darker and skinnier than before, like the rest of us. His hair was dirty and unkempt, and his chin was fringed with the beginning of a beard. But he had the same walk. The same intense stare. When that stare landed on me, I felt the eerie sensation that I'd experienced a hundred times on the island. All at once, I realized that the enemy, the person who had been spying on us, who had severed the neck of the ibis, might very well be looking at me right now.

As for the old man, he was a strange creature. Leaning on a walking stick, he was mostly bald, save the odd tuft of yellow-white hair sprouting above his ears. Moles and freckles mapped a dermatologist's nightmare atop his head, on his shoulders, and along his skeletal arms. When he stepped forward with his stick, he was more spry than I would have guessed. I zeroed in on his filthy hands and feet. In the firelight, I could see that his nails, particularly his toenails, were long and pointy as claws.

The ragged loincloth drooping about the old man's waist looked so ancient it was impossible to know what color it had once been. A beat-up belt held up the loincloth, and from that belt hung a knife sheath and a pair of wire-rim eyeglasses. The glasses were old-fashioned, something you'd find at a flea market or antiques store, maybe even a museum. I noticed that one of the lenses was missing. For some reason those glasses gave me an awful feeling.

"Pablo, are you all right?" Chester asked incredulously. "I can't believe it's you. Where have you been?"

Pablo's expression didn't change as he eyed us, one by one. I could tell that Chester wanted to go to him and embrace him but was holding back out of fear. There was something frightening about Pablo, beyond the obvious changes in his appearance, or the fact that he was standing beside an ancient stranger. I think it had to do with his eyes. At Drake Rosemont, they'd been serious, but open and friendly. Now they were grave.

The old man looked at us and glowered. "Who blew the conch?"

His voice was gravelly, and he had a British accent. Only it didn't sound anything like Rittika's. Hers was highbrow, the old man's raw and unpolished. His jaundice-yellow eyes scanned each of us, but settled on Rittika, who held the huge shell in her hands.

"Only the chief blows the conch," he said.

"Who are you?" she asked, taking a half step closer to her brother.

The old man smiled, revealing a wasteland of a mouth. He had only a couple of teeth left, and they were yellow-brown, stumpy as an old horse's.

"The chief," he replied.

Out of the corner of my eye, I watched Mel take her knife out of her sock. A second later, she had it pointed toward the old man.

"What do you want from us?" she demanded.

Pablo looked at the chief, clearly deferring to him.

"We told you before. Leave this island," the old man spat.

"Why do you want us to leave?" she asked.

His eyes narrowed. "Why? You've eaten my fruit, hunted my pigs, stolen my conchs, taken my . . ."

"We were just trying to survive," Mel interrupted.

"This island is not yours!"

"It's not anybody's."

The old man seemed to be growing angrier. "I fought for this island. I stayed, even after the big liner sailed away. I've been here longer than you've been alive."

"We mean no harm," Mel said, changing tactics and lowering her knife.

At that, Pablo laughed hollowly. "You mean no harm," he repeated sarcastically. "Do you say that to yourselves when you think about Anne Marie's dead body?"

"You know what happened?" Mel asked.

"Of course I know."

"You've seen everything," she said. It wasn't a question.

"What you guys did to Anne Marie at the tar pit—it was the most vicious thing I've ever seen," he said, his bitterness palpable. "You were like animals. No, worse than animals! Because animals at least have a reason for what they do."

Suddenly, a monkey appeared. The same one that was always lurking around. I watched it intently, expecting it to dash into the jungle as it always did. Instead, it ambled up to the old man and sprang into his arms. The man propped the creature on his shoulder, where it perched contentedly, as if that were its usual roost. Ming and Avery shrank back fearfully. Rittika slipped behind her brother.

"Is that why you left?" Mel asked, zeroing in on Pablo. "Because you couldn't stand to be around us anymore?"

"I knew I was better off on my own," he replied coolly.

"Where did you go?"

"I slept in the jungle a couple of days. Then I went to the caves. That was where I met the chief." Pablo glanced at the old man, a glint of adoration in his eyes. "He didn't like me at first; I could tell. But when I told him I didn't mean any harm, he let me be. He even gave me food and water. He was kind . . ."

"I was waiting for you," the old man said. He fished something out of his loincloth and held it up for us to see. It was, of all things, the pilot's glass eye. "When I found the sign, I knew you'd come."

"He's been waiting for someone to help him watch over the island," Pablo explained.

"I've been here a hundred years," the old man said. "All this time—no hunters, no friends, 'cept a monkey or two. My job's to keep others out. But I'm slow now, slower every day . . ."

"When the chief can no longer protect the island, I will," Pablo finished.

A hundred years? No hunters? It was hard to understand what the old man was saying. Harder still to believe it. Clearly, he wasn't in his right mind. Maybe it was old age; maybe it was being marooned on this island, all alone. Talk about going stir-crazy. And yet Pablo gazed at him almost reverently, like Luke Skywalker might look at Yoda.

"The chief has taught me things," Pablo said. "Things I've always wanted to know. Like how to live in nature, surviving, taking only what you need. The chief—all he wants is to live on this island by himself. I can respect that. He doesn't want anyone to mess with it. And he's right. People have a way of destroying everything that's beautiful."

At that he looked directly at Rittika and Rish. "It's funny, we're in this whole new place, this Eden. But you guys are still the same: selfish and destructive. You've never been able to see past yourself, your money, and houses, and vacations. When I used to tell you about the things I believe in, you looked at me like I was crazy. You didn't get it then, and you don't get it now."

"Bro, listen to yourself. What the hell's gotten into you?" Chester asked. "We're your friends."

"You're not my *friends*. You run around the jungle with your spears, yelling about war. You tortured Anne Marie, then let her die. She needed our protection, and all she got was pain. So don't dare try to tell me you're the good guys."

At that, a burst of anger exploded in me. I thought about how worried I'd been about Pablo. I thought about how much

I'd missed him, and how I'd always counted him as a friend. I'd assumed he'd counted me as one, too.

"But you've spilled blood, too," I said. "You killed the ibis—an innocent animal. An *endangered* animal."

In that instant, I saw the old Pablo. Hints of sorrow and regret flashed in his eyes. Although fleeting, there was still a tenderness there as he looked at me. If I were going to be honest with myself, I guess I'd hoped Pablo would be more than a friend.

"What can I say?" he said softly. "There has to be sacrifice to achieve the greater good. You guys started this thing—I'm just trying to finish it."

"Pablo, we're going to leave," Mel said, her voice even and controlled. "I'm sure you've seen the raft."

I wondered why she had chosen this moment to announce our news. Maybe she thought it would calm him down.

"I've seen it. But it's not big enough for all of you."

"That's right," said Rittika, reappearing from behind Rish, still holding the conch. "Some of us want to stay."

"The chief won't allow you to stay. The longer you're here, the more you destroy."

At that, the monkey on the old man's shoulders hissed and jumped to the ground. He began to scamper around Camp Summerbliss, in and out of tents. "He's probably looking for shoes. He's the one who stole Chester's," Pablo said. "He's got a pile of 'em in the caves, from god knows when—and who."

I felt sick thinking about those shoes, and about what had become of their owners. Mel must've been thinking the same thing, for she asked how many others had come to the island.

The old man began to count on his fingers like a child. He got up to nine. "They came on boats," he said. "One or two at a time. Some left right away. But some stayed. I gave 'em a scare." He pointed to his knife sheath, then ran a long, ragged fingernail across his own throat.

Pablo looked at him and nodded. Then he said, "Like I said, sometimes sacrifices must be made. And there will be more sacrifices, if you don't go. *All* of you."

There was no question that it was a threat. I felt simultaneously revolted and mind-blown. I realized that the chief and Pablo finding each other was like a perfect storm. The old man wanted only one thing: to keep the island—*his* island—free of others. Pablo wanted only one thing, too: to protect this vulnerable place of natural wonders. Somehow, these two callings had collided, becoming one and the same, and uniting two unlikely people in the process.

"All right," Rittika said suddenly. "I respect where you're coming from. Maybe you're right. Maybe we should leave." She looked at the old man, then bent her head as if in shame. "I'm sorry for the trouble we caused."

I stared at her dumbfounded. Was the world turning upside down? Rittika was not one to go down without a fight. I had never seen her yield to anyone, least of all to a shriveled old man.

Lifting her head, Rittika looked at her brother, who nodded, then handed the conch to the old man. He clutched it in his bony hands and smirked his decrepit smile. The jungle, once again, went eerily silent.

The chief proceeded to examine the conch. With his attention on the shell, I half expected Rish or Chester to launch a surprise attack, but they didn't. They were probably waiting for Rittika to tell them what to do.

For what seemed like an eternity the old man studied the conch. Then he put it to his lips. The sound that he produced was the loudest we'd heard yet, more thunderous than thunder. Birds squawked and winged into the air. Something small and shadowy skittered past on the ground, disappearing with a squeak into the jungle. We waited nervously, unsure what we were waiting for.

Looking pleased with himself, the old man laughed. Despite his odd appearance, I realized there was something innocent about him—it was almost as if his mind hadn't aged along with his body. He let the shell hang by his side. Then he turned to Pablo to speak. When he opened his mouth, however, he could only gasp.

Suddenly, he dropped the conch and grabbed his throat. His gasps turned to raw, guttural spasms. He stuck out his tongue like a dog. It hung there, skinny and pink, sloppy and strange, saliva dripping off the end, as his eyes rolled back in his head. I took a step back in horror, watching his arms and legs begin to twitch. Even his bad leg jerked about.

One by one, he lost control of every part of his body. I'd

never seen anyone have a seizure before, but I was sure this is what one must look like. The thrashing, flailing, and convulsing. It was madness.

Pablo put his arms around the old man's body from behind, trying to calm him. The monkey screeched wildly. I watched in horror as the chief began to gnaw on his own tongue, turning it to bloody chuck. His eyes had rolled back so far that only the whites were visible.

He looked pathetic, tragic, and possessed all at the same time.

Desperately, Pablo shoved the tongue back into the old man's mouth, but it was too late. It was already bitten in half. The whole scene was a gorefest: spit and blood everywhere, the monkey screeching maniacally from the sidelines, a piece of pink tongue on the ground, everyone stunned quiet except the old man, who tried futilely to breathe and talk as his body shut down.

The last thing I remember before he died was Pablo's expression. He looked like that painting *The Scream* by Edvard Munch, his mouth a perfect O, hands on either side of his face, his uvula visible at the back of his throat. By then, Mel had put the tip of her knife against Pablo's back.

"Don't move," she warned. He was still clutching the chief and didn't look like he was in a position to do anything at all. Rish and Chester pried his arms off the old man and tied his wrists together with vines. The old man slumped onto the ground.

"What just happened?" Avery demanded, tears streaming down her face. Beside her, Ming was bent over, dry-heaving.

I didn't need anyone to explain. And the fact that I already knew how the old man had died made me feel so guilty that I almost dropped to my knees. When Mel looked at me, I couldn't meet her eyes. I could only imagine how she must feel— disappointed and betrayed, as disgusted with me as I was with myself. Her knife might have been pressed to Pablo, but I was pretty sure it was she who felt stabbed in the back.

"I poisoned him," Rittika said simply.

"What? How?" Avery sputtered.

"Remember that little yellow frog? Mel filled syringes with its poison, but I was the one who actually did the deed." She gloated, bending down and patting her sock. "I've had one tucked in here. Thought it might come in handy, and it did." She glanced at me, but I couldn't meet her gaze, either. "Thanks, Sam."

Scornfully, Rittika assessed the chief's body. Then she bent down, plucked the wire eyeglasses from his loincloth, and attached them to the shark's-tooth necklace around her neck. A hunter's trophy. Darkly, she turned her attention to Avery and Ming with a new level of authority.

"Toss him into the ocean," she ordered. "I don't want him on my island anymore."

NINETEEN

TOO MUCH HAD HAPPENED TOO QUICKLY. I COULDN'T think, not even about Pablo and the old man. When Mel said we needed to get some rest and make decisions in the morning, I didn't object.

I watched Rish and Chester tie Pablo's ankles, too. Then they double-checked their knots. Betty asked Pablo if he wanted water or food, if he needed to go to the bathroom. But he wouldn't even look at her, much less speak. Rish and Chester carried him into a tent and laid him down inside. We didn't know what else to do with him.

Hours passed and night fell. As I crawled inside my own tent, I felt more paranoid than ever. It was true that we'd killed the enemy, or who we thought he was. But Rittika had proven to be the real cold-blooded killer. My mind replayed the showdown with the chief and Pablo over and over again. And each time I had the same takeaway. The only person we really needed to fear—the only person we'd *ever* needed to fear—was Rittika.

I edged closer to Mel, acutely aware that she was mad at me. I knew we needed to talk about how I'd told Rittika about the poison. I knew I needed to apologize. Although I was pretty sure Mel would forgive me—she wasn't one to hold a grudge—I wondered if my disloyalty would change our relationship. Maybe after this she'd never trust me again. Maybe she'd always be a little on guard. I wouldn't be able to bear it if she stopped thinking of me as a sister.

"Mel," I whispered. I went to shake her, then heard the steady rhythm of her exhalations. She was sleeping. Damn, I thought. I wanted to get the difficult talk out of the way. But time passed, and pretty soon I fell asleep, too. I dreamt the monkey came back to avenge the old man's death. To chew off our toes and fingers as we slept. Abruptly, I awoke, my heart racing, my body covered in sweat. But nobody was screaming in pain. The night was quiet, almost peaceful, except for the faint sound of Pablo crying.

I wondered if Rittika was listening to him, too. If she was, did she care? I wondered if she'd been lying to me when she'd admitted to having nightmares. I wondered if anything got under her skin.

At dawn I awoke feeling awful. My head pounded. I had a disgusting taste in my mouth, like something had crawled inside and died there. Also, I was disoriented—unsure for a few seconds where I was: Drake Rosemont, my own house, the island? Yes, the island. Once I had my bearings, I can't say I felt any better.

Mel wasn't beside me. Maybe she was out collecting the last of the supplies we'd need for the voyage. I wondered if we would leave the island that day, or stick around a while longer in light of Pablo's return. When I left the tent, I was surprised to see everyone except Mel sitting in a circle around the dying embers of a fire. They were speaking in quiet, conspiratorial voices.

"He must have that disease," Chester whispered. "What's it called? Some Swedish word . . ."

"Stockholm Syndrome," Rish replied.

"Yeah, that's it."

"Is that, like, even a real thing?" asked Avery.

"Yeah, it's real," said Rish. "It's when you start to identify with your captor. You start to think he's doing the right thing."

"Well, that pretty much describes Pablo," Chester said.

"True."

"I don't know about the rest of you, but I don't blame Pablo," Betty said. "The old man got to him while he was vulnerable. Pablo didn't stand a chance."

"No," Rittika objected. "Let's be honest. Pablo wanted to be with the old man. They were like two peas in a pod."

"Does it even matter?" asked Betty. "Look, the old man's dead, but Pablo's still here—and he's one of us. We've gotta help him."

"She's right," said Ming. "We've gotta do something."

"Are you kidding me?" Rittika asked. "You guys are way too forgiving. The old man and Pablo were threatening us. Stalking us. We were basically their *prey*."

"I agree with my sister," said Rish.

"I think we can help Pablo," said Betty. "Rehabilitate him."

"What are we—therapists?" Rittika asked.

"If not help, then what do you propose?"

"Look, he's too far gone. There's nothing we can do."

"What are you saying?" Betty asked, her voice cracking.

"You know what I'm saying."

"No, don't even suggest it! That's so wrong it's beyond wrong. The old man—fine, he had to go. But Pablo, he's our friend."

"*Was* our friend."

"At least give him a chance to explain himself!"

When Rittika sighed, Rish put his hand on her shoulder. "Maybe Betty's right," he said. "Maybe we ought to give him a chance."

Rittika shook her head sulkily. "I don't agree, but if you feel that strongly . . . go ahead."

Chester and Rish looked at each other, then went to get Pablo out of the tent. They untied his feet and helped him up. When he emerged, he was the same as yesterday: pissed off and agitated. He stood there, his back against the bark of a tree, staring at us with contempt.

"I'm gonna give you the benefit of the doubt and untie this," Rish said, untwisting the knots that bound his wrists together. "But don't do anything stupid. Because we can do today what we did yesterday." Pablo glanced at him scornfully, then spit on the ground.

"Do you want something to eat?" Betty asked, her tone accommodating, like she was desperate to make peace. "Or some water? You must be thirsty."

He looked at her and shook his head, his first attempt at communication since the old man's death. I felt a little relieved.

"We don't want to hurt you, but we don't want you to hurt us, either," Betty said gently.

"Don't baby him," warned Rittika, flipping back her hair.

"I'm just trying to be nice."

"He doesn't deserve it."

At that, Pablo glared at Rittika with a hatred so pure it made me recoil. "I wish it was you that got poisoned," he hissed.

She got up and walked over to him, leaning in close, getting in his face. I wasn't sure which of them to worry for more—Rittika or Pablo. "It must have sucked to lose someone you loved."

"The chief called you an evil sow," he retorted, staring into her eyes. "He said we should stick you—stick you like a pig."

"Hey!" Rish said, jumping in. "Do *not* talk about my sister like that."

Pablo gave him a sly, rancorous smile. "Oh, and here comes the sidekick—right on time. What are you so afraid of, Rish? That someone will finally tell the truth about your family?"

At that, Rish lunged forward, shoving Pablo in the chest. Pablo put up his hands, blocking another shove, and continued. "And your father—the Maharaja of India—where's he, Rish? Wasn't he supposed to sweep down in his diamond-encrusted helicopter and save us?" Pablo turned his head, pretending to look around. "Where'd he go?"

"Oh, let him talk," Rittika told her brother. "That's all he has now—words."

Fuming, Rish took a step back. I could see that it took effort. Rage simmered in his eyes, threatening to boil over.

"Words? Yeah, I got more of those," said Pablo. "What I think is that your father spent about three minutes looking for you, then went back to his mansions and Maybachs."

"Keep pushing me, man. You'll regret it," Rish seethed. Then he put his hand in the pocket of his threadbare shorts. He pulled something out—something I didn't recognize at first. It was made of tattered leather. The old man's sheath. I guess Rish, like his sister, had taken a trophy from the kill. With trembling hands, he opened it and held up the knife. It was twice the size of Mel's blade, and twice as formidable.

"If I don't stop, then what?" asked Pablo. "You've always been all talk, dude. It's your sister who calls the shots. You probably don't even know how to use that thing."

"Shut up," said Rish. But as if to reinforce Pablo's point, he stole a look at his sister. She locked eyes with him and shook her head.

"Bingo," Pablo said.

"I said, shut up!" Rish warned, turning to Pablo again. He gripped the knife a little tighter. I didn't think for a second he would use it. Pablo might have been trash-talking, but he was right about Rittika being the boss.

"Honestly, dude, what does it matter what I say? Don't you get it? The chief's gone. It's over. Everything's lost. So you can stop pretending to be a hero. You can go back to who you are."

"You don't know anything about me," Rish cried, his whole body trembling.

For the first time, Pablo took a step forward. The early morning sunlight glinted in his mocking eyes. "Oh, I know a whole lot. Like how you're probably glad we got stuck on this island. Because now you can finally admit it. You and your sister are totally into each other."

It happened so suddenly that I didn't register it at first. Rish, embarrassed and furious, sprang forward and jabbed the knife into Pablo's stomach. One swift play, in and out. Pablo winced and toppled over awkwardly on his side. On the ground he moaned. Blood dripped brightly from his wound, forming a gruesome, dark blot on the waistband of his shorts. A blot that kept growing as the seconds ticked by.

"Oh my god, Rish, what did you do?" Betty whispered.

Pablo began to writhe in agony. He tried to use his own hands to cover up the wound, but there was too much blood, and it was coming so fast. Out of nowhere, Mel appeared. She dropped the fruit she was carrying and knelt down beside him, putting her own hand against the incision, desperately trying to staunch the flow. Alas, it kept coming, dripping wetly around her fingers, trickling onto the mossy earth. I began to wobble, feeling the same dizzy, disbelieving sensation as when Anne Marie had fallen into the tar pit. In that instant, I couldn't look at Pablo's face because then I'd know what was happening was real. I could only look at the blood. I'd seen enough of that on the island to last me the rest of my life.

The color draining from his face, Rish dropped the knife. In the blink of an eye, he went from enraged to disbelieving. He hovered around Mel helplessly, watching the blood—Pablo's very life—pour out faster than we could think. Watching everything unfold, I realized with sickening certainty that Pablo was going to die. And I knew that his death was the most barbaric one of all, because we'd all played a part in it, one way or another.

After Pablo stopped breathing, Rish sat down next to him on the ground, or rather collapsed. No one spoke. No words felt adequate.

"You were right to do it," Rittika said at length, breaking the silence.

"No," Rish whispered.

"Yes. He pushed you—he pushed you too far. It wasn't murder. It was . . . it was . . ." She groped in vain for the word. "Justice," she said at last.

At that, Rish hunched over and started sobbing.

Rittika tiptoed around the puddle of blood and put her arm around him. She whispered, "It's all right," over and over again, but he shrugged her off. Rebuffed, she wiped away the tears that had gathered in the corners of her own eyes. After a minute or two, she straightened her back and lifted her chin, looking more composed. More like the Rittika we were all used to seeing.

"Maybe this is what had to happen," she said, looking at us all. "Now there is no one else against us. We can finally be here without worrying. We can *live*. Rish and I have traveled everywhere, to the best places in the world, and none of them beats this island. I can promise you that. Isn't that right, Rish?"

He looked away, his face still streaked with tears.

"*This* is where we should be," she continued, her voice a little hollow. "We'll make our own rules, without anyone telling us what's right or wrong. We'll live how we want—for as long as we want."

She ended breathlessly, her eyes roaming hungrily until they settled on Avery, the one she knew, without a doubt, she could persuade. Avery licked her lips, seeming to consider the enormity of the decision before her. Or perhaps she'd already made the decision and was only basking in the rare glow of Rittika's absolute, undivided attention.

"I'll stay as long as you do," she replied.

Of course. It was exactly what we knew she'd say. Avery had always done whatever Rittika wanted her to do—robotically and automatically. Why would now be any different?

Together, the two girls turned their attention next to Ming, another link in Rittika's chain.

Feeling their eyes on her, Ming began to scratch nervously at one of the many mosquito bites dotting her legs.

"Okay, I guess. Me too," she said weakly.

Rittika smiled at her. "You hear that, Rish? No one holds this against you. They know it had to be done. It had to be done for this island to be ours."

It was as if they'd already forgotten about Pablo. All of them. Even Chester and Betty were focused on Rittika, absorbing her words, submitting to her point of view. And I guess that made sense. I remembered what I'd learned about ants and damselflies. About all creatures. Some dominate, others submit, and still others die. It was the way of nature. At Drake Rosemont, we'd pretended to be outside those savage rules. We'd pretended to be civilized.

We'd lied to ourselves.

Mel and I told the others we were leaving immediately. After this, I couldn't imagine staying. Most of our classmates just stared at us apathetically. Only Betty expressed concern. She worried about our safety. She talked about how fragile the previous rafts had been. Was ours really any better?

The truth was, I didn't know.

Rittika was concerned, too, but that's only because she thought we'd rat out her brother.

"We wouldn't tell," I promised her, meaning it.

"You can't admit what Rish did. What any of us did . . . ," she whispered, her face close to mine.

"I won't."

"Swear to me—as a Gold."

"I swear," I said, putting my hand over my heart.

"But what about Mel?"

"She won't tell either. If we make it back, we'll just say Pablo and Anne Marie didn't survive the crash—just like Warren and Jeremiah didn't. In a way, none of us survived it, did we?" I looked at her meaningfully. "We're different people now."

She let that penetrate, then told me to wait a moment; she

had something for me. She disappeared into her tent, returning with the giant conch, the one that had changed everything. "For you," she said, trying to hand it to me. "For good luck."

"I don't need luck," I told her, shaking my head, repelled by her offer. "I have Mel."

My best friend and I took a little longer to collect the rest of what we needed, including various herbs and medicines from the jungle, and to say our good-byes. During that time, Betty approached me.

"Can't you guys take a few more days?" she asked. "To think it through?"

"I feel as strongly about going as you do about staying."

"Do you really?"

The way she looked at me, I knew what she meant—that Mel and I were ludicrous to think we had any chance of getting to safety. That when you compared our schlumpy, tacked-together little raft to the deep and boundless ocean, things looked pretty bleak. I guess she just wanted me to admit it. But I wouldn't.

"Betty, when we get there, we'll send for help."

"Whatever," she replied stiffly.

Once again, I wanted to yell at her. To get her to see reason. I wanted to share what Mel had said—about people becoming unhinged, about terrible things happening. Of course they would. Pablo and Anne Marie were already proof of that. "Tell me," I said, more hotly than I intended to, "are you really ready to celebrate your eighteenth birthday here? What about your thirtieth? Tell me, are you ready to die here?"

She took a deep breath and looked away, but not before I saw the doubt in her eyes. "I guess someone has to go," she admitted. "I just wish it wasn't you."

Hesitating, she put her arms around me and we hugged each other tightly. We didn't mention the obvious, that we might never see each other again. But the truth was, a part of me was already gone, adrift at sea. I felt it was my destiny to be aboard that raft with Mel. If she and I made it to safety, then we'd make it back together. And if we went down, well, we'd do that together, too. We were sisters, after all. United till the end.

Mel insisted we go over what we were bringing one last time. We discussed each item, one by one. As I put them into a backpack, I finally got the chance to say how I was sorry—for telling Rittika about the hidden syringes, for everything. She just shrugged. "I don't blame you. Not at all. Rittika can be very persuasive."

"But I let you down," I said.

"Then we're even. Because I let you down, too."

"What?"

"After the crash, when we found each other, I told you everything was going to be okay . . ."

I couldn't help but smile. "Let's just agree not to do it again—disappoint each other, I mean," I said.

"Deal," she said, and we shook on it.

At some point, Ming and Avery approached us tentatively. They looked uncomfortable, glancing all around, worried that someone was watching. Then Avery took my wrist and squeezed it hard, willing me to listen.

"I know Rittika wouldn't want us to say this," she whispered. "But please don't forget about us, Samantha Mishra. Don't you dare."

Mel boarded the raft first. Then I, too, climbed on, and our classmates pushed us out beyond the shallows. Rish and Chester swam up to their necks before letting go. Rittika stood alone on the beach. When I waved at her, she raised one hand briefly, and I got a bittersweet feeling, as if I'd lost and gained something at the same time.

I just had one more thing to do. It had to do with what was in my hand: the glass eye. The thing I'd taken from the old man. *My* talisman. I thumbed it one last time—memorizing its cool, smooth shape—before hurling it as far as I could. It made a satisfying little splash somewhere in the sea. Then Mel and I looked at each other, knowing that it was time.

I took an oar and began to paddle into deeper ocean. The boys stayed behind the barrier of the reef, in the tranquil turquoise water. Mel tried to stabilize a corner of the shade tarp, which had come loose.

Because there was little wind, the sails couldn't do their job, not yet. But I rowed steadily, making slow progress against the waves, which instinctively pushed us back toward the shore, toward our classmates and all that had been. It felt strange when the island finally began to shrink, receding little by little, my classmates fading into tiny dots. After a few minutes, I couldn't see them at all, and the island was just a dark smudge on a blue canvas. I wondered if someday the details would fade: The sounds and shapes, the textures and tastes. The buzz of mosquitoes and the endless green. I didn't know. The only thing I was sure of was that I'd never forget my classmates, especially the ones I'd lost.

Mel and I were quiet, nothing to say, nothing to hear but the sloshing waves and the whistling wind. Together, we looked back, watching the island till it grew fainter and hazier, till I couldn't quite be sure it was still there.

ACKNOWLEDGMENTS

For her patience, perseverance, and keen insight, I offer deepest gratitude to Marly Rusoff, who always believed in this book and fearlessly shepherded it through numerous iterations. Special thanks to members of her team, especially Julie Mosow and Michael Radulescu, who did crucial work behind the scenes. At every stage Anamika Bhatnagar, editor extraordinaire, provided perceptive feedback and suggestions, improving the story immeasurably. Megan Peace, multitalented associate editor, never failed to go above and beyond the call of duty. I am indebted to Joy Simpkins, one of the best copy editors I've ever had the privilege of working with, and Mary Claire Cruz, a designer who magically transforms words and ideas into arresting visuals. I'd like to acknowledge Leo Nickolls, surely among today's most talented book jacket artists. Finally, I couldn't have written this novel without the love and support of my family. Thank you for being my bedrock.

—C.P.

ABOUT THE AUTHOR

CHANDRA PRASAD is the author of several critically acclaimed novels for adults, including *On Borrowed Wings*, a historical drama set in the early twentieth century, and *Death of a Circus,* which *Booklist* called "richly textured [and] packed with glamour and grit." She is also the originator and editor of *Mixed,* an anthology of short stories on the multiracial experience. Her shorter works have appeared in *The Wall Street Journal*, *The New York Times*, and *The New York Times Magazine,* among others. A graduate of Yale University, Chandra lives and works in Connecticut. Visit her online at chandraprasad.com.